‖‖‖‖‖‖‖‖‖‖‖‖‖‖‖
✍ **W9-AZM-149**

"I know you're crazy about the baby."

"I am!" she confessed. "But that's not the problem."

"Then what is?" Even in the semi-dark interior of the cab, his eyes blazed a hot blue. *The problem is you, Mr. Broderick. I think I've fallen in love with you, and you only see me as a live-in nanny.*

"It's inevitable he would get attached to me. It would be a wrench for him when I have to leave. Cruel, in fact. He deserves to have someone around on a permanent basis, not just a month or two."

"I couldn't agree more, and I have a solution. In fact I would have suggested it in the beginning. But first I needed to find out if there was a man in your life."

"I don't understand."

"Marry me."

Captain Howard Stansbury of the U.S. Topographical
engineers, who surveyed the valley of the Great Salt Lake
in 1849, reported, "This valley is called Tuilla Valley."
(sounds like Two-Willa).

The name comes from the Shoshoni Indian Language
and is a Gosiute tongue variant, named for the Bear family,
a Gosiute Indian family, some of whose members still
reside in Tooele today.

Books by Rebecca Winters

HARLEQUIN ROMANCE®
3632—THE BILLIONAIRE AND THE BABY*
3601—HIS VERY OWN BABY*

*Bachelor Dads trilogy

Don't miss any of our special offers. Write to us at the
following address for information on our newest releases.

Harlequin Reader Service
U.S.: 3010 Walden Ave., P.O. Box 1325, Buffalo, NY 14269
Canadian: P.O. Box 609, Fort Erie, Ont. L2A 5X3

THE BABY
DISCOVERY
Rebecca Winters

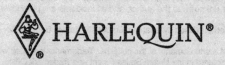

TORONTO • NEW YORK • LONDON
AMSTERDAM • PARIS • SYDNEY • HAMBURG
STOCKHOLM • ATHENS • TOKYO • MILAN • MADRID
PRAGUE • WARSAW • BUDAPEST • AUCKLAND

If you purchased this book without a cover you should be aware
that this book is stolen property. It was reported as "unsold and
destroyed" to the publisher, and neither the author nor the
publisher has received any payment for this "stripped book."

To Janet and George, with love and gratitude
for their invaluable help.

ISBN 0-373-03639-6

THE BABY DISCOVERY

First North American Publication 2001.

Copyright © 2000 by Rebecca Winters.

All rights reserved. Except for use in any review, the reproduction or
utilization of this work in whole or in part in any form by any electronic,
mechanical or other means, now known or hereafter invented, including
xerography, photocopying and recording, or in any information storage
or retrieval system, is forbidden without the written permission of the
publisher, Harlequin Enterprises Limited, 225 Duncan Mill Road,
Don Mills, Ontario, Canada M3B 3K9.

All characters in this book have no existence outside the imagination of
the author and have no relation whatsoever to anyone bearing the same
name or names. They are not even distantly inspired by any individual
known or unknown to the author, and all incidents are pure invention.

This edition published by arrangement with Harlequin Books S.A.

® and TM are trademarks of the publisher. Trademarks indicated with
® are registered in the United States Patent and Trademark Office, the
Canadian Trade Marks Office and in other countries.

Visit us at www.eHarlequin.com

Printed in U.S.A.

CHAPTER ONE

A FREEZING gust of wind caused Zane Broderick to turn up the collar of his sheepskin jacket. An early December snowstorm had blown in, making for poor visibility in this remote wilderness.

It was the "lake effect" that gave Tooele its reputation for severe winter weather. Forty minutes from Salt Lake, the tiny Utah town received an overabundance of moisture due to its proximity to the Great Salt Lake.

Tonight he felt a whiteout coming on. The kind where livestock froze and all transportation came to a standstill. By tomorrow morning the conditions would be perfect for the engineering team to do an experimental, driverless winter test run of the new prototype magnetic levitation train he'd designed.

As soon as he'd given one more inspection to this last section of forged track for any unforeseen problems, he could call it a night.

Blizzard conditions made it impossible to rely on his eyes without help. He pulled the heavy-duty flashlight from the back of his truck where he'd covered his equipment with a tarp.

The wind drove the snow so hard, his footsteps disappeared with every step he took alongside the platformed structure housing the twelve miles of seamless track.

Twenty minutes later he was satisfied that the workmanship looked slick-as-a-whistle, as his father would say. He came to the last hundred feet, carefully shining his light down inside to make certain he'd covered every square inch.

While he'd been out here, the wind, strengthened in force, pelted him with icy shards. At times its moaning sounds rose in pitch, imitating an animal's cry.

Zane began to think a cougar foraging for food must have come down from the nearby mountains and had picked up his scent.

He made a last scan with the light, then froze.

Something about the size of a sack of flour was lying in the middle of the track wrapped in a snow-covered cloth. It was hard to make out details with white stuff swirling all around him.

He heard another cry, more distinct this time. What the devil?

In the next second he vaulted inside to see what it was. As he drew closer, he could have sworn the material moved.

A grimace marred his features. Had some deranged lunatic decided to dispose of a cat in this fashion?

Hunkering down, he carefully removed one edge of the thin cotton material. After pointing the light on it, he let out a gasp of sheer disbelief.

A newborn baby without a stitch of clothing on!

It made another infant cry.

Good Lord. The little boy was on the verge of freezing to death!

Tears of rage filled Zane's eyes. If he hadn't decided to inspect this end portion of track one more time...

Setting down the light, he whipped off his jacket. Carefully he placed the baby against the sheepskin lining and wrapped it up like a cocoon. All the while he prayed the warmth from his own body would ward of hypothermia.

Without a second to lose, he climbed back out with his precious bundle and started running.

The tears continued to run down his cheeks. They froze to his skin but he wasn't cognizant of anything except the tiny life that would have died from exposure, if not from...

He couldn't think about the other horrific scenarios flooding his mind. He refused!

The truck was two miles away, but it felt like a hundred. The baby could die before he got it to a hospital.

Suppressed memories of Zane's twin brother drowning in San Francisco Bay years ago came back with gut-wrenching clarity.

Please God. Let this baby live.

Julie Becker, the other registered nurse on duty in the emergency room at the small Oquirrh Mountains Medical Center, came into the cubicle where Meg Richins was setting up a morphine drip on a migraine sufferer.

"It's pretty quiet, Meg," she whispered. "I thought I'd run across the street for some fresh cappuccino. The coffee around here is ghastly. Do you want anything?"

"I don't think so, but thanks anyway," Meg whispered back. "Let's just be grateful we're on the night shift. After the storm is over in the morning, there will be a steady stream of casualties."

"Don't I know it, and we'll both be in our apartments sound asleep! But alone in our beds," she added jokingly.

Meg smiled, but it really wasn't funny.

"See you in a few minutes."

When she left, Meg looked down at her patient. "How's the nausea, Mrs. Pope?"

"It's not too bad yet."

"Let me know if it gets worse and I'll tell Dr. Tingey. We can give you something for it."

"I'm allergic to a lot of things."

"I can see that on your chart. Don't worry. I hate a bad reaction as much as anyone. I promise we'll do everything in our power to make sure you don't suffer any additional discomfort."

A few years ago, after the operation to remove Meg's ovaries, she'd become deathly ill on her first injection of a normal painkiller for that kind of surgery. Since then she'd learned great respect for her patients' fears in that department.

After drawing the curtain for privacy, she walked over to the desk where their intense new resident, Dr. Parker, was writing a prescription for an outgoing patient who'd come in with a broken arm.

She waited until he was finished.

"Yes, Meg?"

"Do you know where Dr. Tingey is?" Meg knew it was wrong of her, but there were some cases where she would rather deal with the seasoned, mellow head of the ER.

"Over in X-ray for the moment. What do you need?"

"This is a list of drugs Mrs. Pope is allergic to. She's nauseated and I'm afraid it's going to get worse. I thought we should be prepared."

He studied it for a minute. "I'll go in and talk to her."

Somehow Meg knew he would say that. One of the new breed of doctors, he always questioned everything the patients said, as if their input wasn't credible. She wondered if he treated his wife the same way, then chastised herself for being unprofessional.

Dr. Tingey was so different, Meg was spoiled. She not only had the greatest respect for his medical expertise, she loved him for his wonderful bedside manner with the patients who adored him.

On more than one occasion she'd heard him say he'd seen everything in his forty years of practice. In that amount of time he'd learned to listen, and truly cared about people. Those qualities alone made him the greatest doctor around as far as she was concerned. Dr. Parker would do well to emulate him.

A slight draft in the room brought Meg's head in the direction of the double doors leading to the entrance of the ER. She assumed it was Julie returning from the convenience store.

Instead her gaze fell on a tall, lean male in his mid-thirties rushing toward her in a snow-covered cowboy hat, jeans and a plaid flannel shirt, but no winter coat. He was clutching something wrapped in his arms.

"Quick! Help me! The baby was left out in the blizzard to die!" The man sounded absolutely frantic.

The word "baby" galvanized her into action. "Come with me." She hurried down to a room marked Infant ICU. "Right in here. Lay the baby on this counter."

While he did her bidding, she switched on the warmer of the specially equipped cribs to treat hypothermia, then undid the rust-colored jacket covering the baby. A tiny head with a dusting of dark hair appeared.

It was a newborn boy! Meg's professional eye looked him over. The umbilical cord still needed trimming.

His naked, shivering body had been wrapped in a thin, blood-stained cotton receiving blanket. He had an unhealthy pallor. She felt for a pulse. It was alarmingly weak, as were its infant cries. When she pressed on the skin of his upper arm, she noted decreased capillary refill.

Who could have done such a thing to a human being, her heart cried in fury.

Swallowing her sobs she whispered, "You precious little darling. Let's get you warmed up."

With the utmost care she lifted him from the counter and placed him unclothed on his back inside the crib. The quiver of his baby chin exaggerated his total helplessness, wringing another inner convulsion from Meg.

"I'll get the doctor," she murmured to the rugged stranger who hovered anxiously nearby. With one covert glance she read pain in his expression as he stared at the miniscule lump of humanity struggling for life.

To her relief, Dr. Tingey had returned from X-ray. As soon as she told him the situation, he followed her to the room where she'd put the baby.

After nodding to the man standing next to the crib, he proceeded to examine the infant.

"This little tyke isn't more than a couple of hours old. Where did you find him?"

"On the train track," came the thick-toned response. Meg moaned at the same time Dr. Tingey grimaced. "I was doing a last-minute inspection of the end section when I heard a cry.

"The second I realized it was a baby, I brought it

here as fast as I could. Is it going to live?" His deep voice sounded haunted.

"We're going to do everything in our power to make certain it does," he assured him in a calm tone.

Two years of working in the ER had taught Meg how to read the expression on Dr. Tingey's face. When one eyebrow arched higher than the other, it meant the victim's medical condition was precarious, but no one else knew that.

"Set up an IV to start the antibiotics and fluid bolus. Then call the lab. I want a full workup, blood cultures, et cetera. Tell Julie to phone the sheriff's office. We have a Baby Doe."

"I'll get right on it."

Meg hurried to do his bidding. It was just as she'd feared. The infant had suffered blood loss during birth. No telling where the delivery had taken place. Considering the raging storm outside, she didn't think she could bear to hear the tragic details, even if they were ever to come to light.

Within fifteen minutes everything possible was being done to stabilize the baby. Meg stood by to monitor the speed of the drip and get more IV bags ready if needed. Dr. Tingey finished trimming and cleaning the cord to make it sterile.

He'd told the stranger he could wait out in the small reception area if he wanted. But the other man insisted he would remain in the room.

It touched Meg's heart that he would show this kind of concern for an abandoned baby. Unfortunately she'd seen too many cases where the natural parent seemed to have no nurturing instincts whatsoever.

Soon she heard voices in the hall and then a police

officer came into the room. He nodded to everyone before his gaze went to the stranger.

"I'm Officer Brown assigned to this case. You're the man who found the baby?"

"That's right."

"What's the name, Sir?"

"Zane Broderick."

"Age?"

"Thirty-four."

"Do you live around here?"

"Yes—1017 Parkway."

"Phone?"

"My number is 734-9812."

"What's your occupation?"

"I'm a mechanical engineer."

"Tell me what happened."

"My crew and I are performing a test on a new maglev train in the morning."

Meg blinked. She'd heard about the exciting project when one of the engineers who'd been involved came in to be treated for a gash on his leg a few months earlier. She'd ridden on a bullet train similar to the type they were building when she'd gone to Japan on a trip with some fellow nurses after graduation.

"I was checking the last section of track for any last-minute problems when I saw a bundle in the middle of it, covered in snow. I thought it was a cat crying until I opened it and found the baby inside, barely alive. It was wrapped in a cloth." He pointed to the cotton blanket still lying inside the jacket.

The officer peered at the bloodstains. "Is this track the one on the west side of town where a large building has been erected at one end?"

"Yes."

"I've seen it."

"I wrapped the baby in my coat and ran for my truck. It was parked two miles up the track. Then I drove straight here."

"Do you know what time it was when you found the baby?"

"Forty-five minutes ago."

"Is that your white Chevy V8 out there in the emergency parking?"

"Yes."

"Give me the names and addresses of a couple of your crew, please."

"Rod Stigler and Martin Driscoll. They live at the Doxey apartments on Conover Street. Number 10 and 14."

"Okay. Thanks for your cooperation. I'm going to have to ask you to remain here until another officer from the station comes over to deal with the evidence and get a blood sample from you."

The policeman turned to Dr. Tingey, but his gaze included Meg. "Don't touch the blanket or the coat. In the meantime, if you should learn anything that could help us trace the birthmother or father, call the station. I'll be in touch."

"Is it routine to be given the third degree?" Mr. Broderick demanded quietly after the officer had left the room. Meg could feel his anger.

"I'm afraid even the good Samaritan is suspect until proven otherwise. As far as the police are concerned this could be a case of attempted murder," Dr. Tingey murmured.

"The problem is, there have been too many instances in the past where the person who found an abandoned newborn turned out to be connected to it in some way. But normally it's a teenage couple who can't deal with the fact that they've become parents. They'll do anything to get rid of it."

Meg shuddered.

"Be patient. The truth will come out soon enough. Looking on the positive side, if this little guy continues to hold his own, there will come a day when he'll want to thank you for saving his life.

"I'd like to thank you now for your quick action. The body warmth from your coat obviously helped preserve him." Dr. Tingey shook the other man's hand.

"Meg?" he called over his shoulder. "Keep the IV going. I've got to check on a head injury patient, then I'll be back." He left the room.

Under the circumstances, Meg couldn't help but admire the kind way Dr. Tingey had tried to put the stranger at ease. He knew how unsettling it must be for Mr. Broderick whose good deed had fallen under suspicion.

"You look like you could use a cup of coffee. Can I get you some?"

His gaze was still riveted to the baby. He seemed deep in thought. "If it wouldn't be too much trouble, I'd appreciate it."

"Not at all. Why don't you bring that stool in the corner over to the crib and sit down while you watch the baby. I'll be back in a moment."

When she returned a few minutes later, she discovered he'd followed her suggestion. In the process he'd removed the well-worn cowboy hat which had been set on the counter next to his coat. Beneath the brightness of the overhead light, his medium-cropped dark-blond hair gleamed with health.

It surprised her to realize they'd both been living in town and she'd never seen him before. Lines of character defining a face burnished by the sun added to his masculine appeal. The combination of his six-foot-three height and well-honed physique made him a rarity among the male of the species. In Tooele, she hadn't known such a man existed...

"Here's your coffee."

"Thank you." He took it from her hands. In that brief moment when he'd looked up, she'd glimpsed a flash of blue. The man was even more attractive than she'd first realized.

"Hi, Meg." The lab technician breezed in with her cart.

"How are you, Angela?" The mother of three was always cheerful.

"Can't complain. Word has spread around the clinic that we have a Baby Doe." She put on sterile gloves, then placed her hands inside the holes of the crib to get started.

"Oh—isn't he sweet!" As she began drawing blood from the baby's heels she said, "With those cheeks, he looks like a chipmunk."

Meg smiled. "My words exactly. He's the most precious thing I've ever seen."

But she noticed that Zane Broderick continued to wear a pained expression throughout the procedure. For someone who'd never laid eyes on the baby until he'd found him on the track, the man seemed exceptionally attached to the child.

Maybe it was because the miracle of birth had happened only hours before its discovery and the crisis had managed to tug at his parental instincts. In some men those feelings were very strong. If that was the case, Meg could well understand his reaction.

Since she'd discovered the tiny infant wrapped inside the man's coat, the powerful drive to mother the child she would never be able to conceive had been given a real workout.

By the time the technician had finished her job, it was time for Meg to start another IV. Mr. Broderick leaned closer to the crib.

"Do you think the baby looks any better yet?"

I wish I could tell you yes, but I can't. "He's holding his own, which means he's a fighter."

"In other words, there's a good chance he might not make it."

His tormented tone alarmed her. "Give him a little more time. Babies are more resilient than you might imagine."

"I wouldn't know." He downed the rest of his coffee.

She checked the thermostat on the warmer to be sure it was maintaining a constant temperature, then reached for his empty cup. "I'll dispose of that." On her way over to the waste bin, two policemen entered the room.

"Mr. Broderick? If you'll come with me."

The stranger's jaw hardened. Meg shared in his frustration as he got up from the stool and was forced to follow one of the officers out the door. The other officer placed the cotton blanket and sheepskin parka in bags for the forensics lab to examine.

Putting on sterile gloves, Meg walked back to the crib. Her heart ached for this baby who'd been deprived of his mother and desperately needed to be held. She reached inside the holes and grasped his tiny hands, trying to infuse him with all the love she would have poured out on her own baby. The one she would never have...

"You're the sweetest boy I've ever seen. So strong and brave. The man who saved you thinks you are, too. He'll be back. You're not alone in the world, little precious."

"Am I allowed to make a phone call now?" Zane demanded in suppressed anger, rolling down his shirtsleeve over the gauze the technician had taped to his inner elbow.

The officer nodded. "Of course. Thanks for cooperating. We'll get your coat back to you within twenty-four hours."

After the policeman and technician had left the emergency room cubicle, Zane pulled out his cell phone. First he called Martin. Following the brief explanation, he asked his assistant to inform the rest of the crew that the test run for tomorrow needed to be postponed for a couple of days. He'd get back to him later.

As soon as they'd said goodbye, he rang Dominic Giraud at his apartment in Laramie, Wyoming. If he didn't answer, then Zane would phone Alik Jarman who lived nearby. Both men were his best friends. Together the three of them were making the maglev project a reality.

This test was the critical one. He knew they'd be upset when they heard it had to be put off for another day or two, but circumst—

"Hello?"

"Hannah?" Dom's wife was a sweetheart.

"Zane! Dominic and Alik were just talking about you."

"Are they still there?"

"Yes."

"Put them both on, will you? I've got something important to tell them."

"Of course. Just a minute."

He could hear happy sounds in the background. In his mind's eye he pictured the small apartment bulging at the seams with both couples and their children assembled in the front room. At the odd time like this, Zane experienced a disquieting emptiness he didn't like to acknowledge, not when his bachelor status had served him perfectly well all these years.

"*Mon vieux*—" His French friend often used the endearment in addressing him and Alik. Right now Zane felt like he was an old man. "Is everything ready for tomorrow?"

"We've been watching the weather channel," Alik broke in on the other line. "You're being blasted with snow right now. Exactly what we wanted for the test run in the morning!"

Zane gripped the phone a little tighter. "I'm afraid the test has to be postponed. That's why I'm calling."

After a slight pause, "What happened?" The disappointment in Dom's voice was tangible.

"It has nothing to do with the train's mechanics."

"Then there's something wrong with *you*," Alik surmised, his tone full of concern.

He sucked in his breath. "You're not going to believe this, but the track has been taped off as a crime scene."

"*What?*" both men interjected at the same time.

"That's right. At the moment I'm the chief suspect

in an attempted murder case. As we speak, I'm in the ER in Tooele where I've just been fingerprinted by the police. They took a blood sample. I've been warned not to leave town until further notice. Oh yes, they'll give me back my parka after the crime lab has examined it."

"It sounds like you need an attorney. Alik and I will phone New York as soon as we hang up."

Thank God for choice friends.

"I appreciate the backing, you two. If it comes to that, I'll let you know. But this is an entirely different situation than you're imagining. Just hear me out."

For the next little while Zane told them everything that had happened. "You should have seen the little guy with only a thin cotton blanket for protection in that blizzard. An animal could have come along. If we'd done that test tomorrow—" Zane was so choked up, he couldn't talk.

"Good Lord," Alik muttered.

"How old did you say he was?"

"An hour maybe."

"Mon Dieu."

"Everything possible is being done for him here, but no one's guaranteeing anything." Not even the attractive nurse who'd brought him coffee had tried to paint a rosy picture. That pretty well said it all.

"How in the hell could the police think you had anything to do with it when you're the one who brought the baby in?"

"According to the doctor, more often than not that person is an accessory to the crime or has knowledge of it. So until the police track down the mother and anyone else involved, I won't be off the hook."

"We're flying to Salt Lake tomorrow, *mon ami.*

Because of the snow, it will probably have to be a late afternoon flight.''

"There's no need to take you away from your families.''

"We're coming,'' Alik declared.

When Zane heard that note of finality in their voices, he knew there was no arguing with them. In truth, he was glad they had insisted. He could use their support at a time like this.

"We'll phone you when we're in the car on the way to Tooele.''

He swallowed hard. "Thanks, guys. It means more than you know.''

Anxious to check on the baby's condition, he clicked off and left the cubicle for the Infant ICU.

While Dr. Parker listened to the baby's heart, Meg charted its fluid intake and output on the computer.

"This is a pretty sick baby.''

"I know,'' she murmured, hating to hear the words. Dr. Tingey always kept those kinds of thoughts to himself. Unfortunately, he'd gone home and left Dr. Parker in charge.

He pulled the ends of the stethoscope out of his ears and turned to Meg. "What's your take on the man who brought it in?''

"What do you mean?'' she played dumb.

"You have to admit that without prior knowledge, the chances of anyone finding Baby Doe where he did on a night like tonight are a zillion to one.''

"I don't understand your point.''

"His story is too far-fetched to be believed. When it all comes out, we'll probably learn it was his girlfriend who tried to get rid of it at home, and he suffered a last-minute attack of conscience."

Dr. Parker had never been her favorite person. His remark just now alienated her even more. No sooner had he gone out the door than she felt another presence in the ICU.

"Is that what you think, too?"

The stranger's deep, unforgettable voice brought Meg's head around to receive the full brunt of brilliant blue eyes alive with pain.

Horrified he'd overheard Dr. Parker's comment she said, "I'm sorry, Mr. Broderick. Would you repeat the question?"

He stood there with his hands on his hips in a purely masculine stance. "Your diplomacy does you great credit, Ms. Richins."

For a moment she'd forgotten about the name tag attached to the pocket of her lab coat. Her face went warm. "Please don't mind what he said. At times no one is immune to the stress of the ER."

"I could go along with that if this place resembled a war zone. But it's as quiet as a tomb around here tonight."

He had a point.

"Dr. Parker has three children of his own. I'm assuming it was the baby's plight that caused him to venture a negative opinion about you."

"Apparently it's shared by a majority of people. Why not you?"

The pointed question caught her off guard.

She could hardly tell him it was the haunted sound of his voice, the look of torment in his eyes when he'd rushed in the ER crying out for help, that had decided her.

"I've always considered a person innocent until proven guilty."

There was a slight pause. "It's nice to know I have one person on my side."

"Two," she amended in the next breath. At his questioning look she said, "You're forgetting the baby."

CHAPTER TWO

"YOU mean Johnny?"

She blinked. *Johnny?*

"I abhor calling him Baby Doe," came the explanation.

"So do I," she said in a tremulous voice. "John's my father's name. I love it. Just don't let anyone else hear you use it. They would jump to the wrong conclusion."

"It will be our secret."

Though what he'd said implied a certain intimacy, she knew they were just words on his part.

"I heard the doctor tell you he's sick," Mr. Broderick added. "I take it he wasn't talking about hypothermia."

She shook her head. "No. The baby has an infection. We'll give him antibiotics for as long as the blood culture comes back positive."

"What else is wrong with him?"

"He's lost blood. That means he's missing vital nutrients we're feeding him through the IV."

"The guy's so tiny. Do you think he's premature?"

The questions fired one after the other reminded her of a brand-new father who needed constant reassurance.

"Probably. But under the circumstances, five pounds is a good weight. Until his lungs are more developed, we'll continue the oxygen to help him breathe.'' She bit her lip. "Thank heaven you found him!"

"I've been doing a lot of that for the last little while," he muttered, his whole attention focused on the baby. He didn't act or sound like he was going to leave anytime soon.

"Excuse me for a moment."

Julie stopped Meg on the way to the lounge area. "I got a good look at the Adonis who brought in Baby Doe," she whispered. "He's a living, breathing miracle!"

"I agree," Meg murmured back. *Unless I'm no judge of character, he's even more exceptional on the inside.*

"It isn't fair!" the vivacious blond nurse whined. "I step outside for five minutes and the only excitement to happen around here in months takes place without me."

"Tell you what. Wait here while I get him a chair, and you can take it to him. The stool's a backbreaker."

"You mean he's not leaving yet?" Her blue eyes lit up in anticipation.

"I'm not sure. He's very anxious about J—the baby," she stammered.

In a matter of seconds Meg returned with one of the comfortable canvas-backed chairs. "I'll keep an eye on Mrs. Pope while you monitor the baby's progress."

Julie smiled with satisfaction. "You're just too good to be true," she sang the song near Meg's ear before wheeling away with the chair.

It was better to let Julie take over in there. She was a natural flirt. If Mr. Broderick turned out to be single and available, the two ought to hit it off without problem.

As for the baby, Meg already felt an attachment to him that went way beyond the norm.

She'd always loved babies and had dreamed of a large family of her own one day. But since she'd learned she could never give birth, it seemed like her problem was all she ever thought about. Especially when her older brother and sister were both married and had children.

Her gynecologist had suggested she get a dog to love. Unfortunately there was a "no pets" rule at the apartment she shared with a dental hygienist, Debbie Lignell. But after her response to the baby, maybe she ought to start thinking about moving to a place where animals were allowed.

By the time she went off the shift at five-thirty a.m., Debbie would be getting ready for work. Meg could broach the subject, but her friend wouldn't like it. Their apartment was a convenient half block away from the dentist's office.

Perhaps the best thing to do was let Debbie advertise for a new roommate so Meg could find a place of her own.

Maybe now would be the best time to move back to Salt Lake. There were plenty of nursing jobs available. If she couldn't get her old floor position back at Emigration Hospital, there were a lot of other hospitals in the Salt Lake Valley. As for apartments that accepted pets, it wouldn't be a problem. What she needed was a new reason to get up in the morning...

Since her operation, she'd avoided dating. That way she didn't have to explain that she could never bear a child and that the guy would be wasting his time with her.

The last man she'd been interested in was a pilot she'd met at an N.B.A. game featuring the Jazz and the Lakers. Once the two of them got talking, it appeared he liked some of the same outdoor activities she loved.

But they'd only been dating a couple of weeks when he was unexpectedly transferred to Atlanta. He'd wanted her to fly out there for a visit. But by then she had developed female problems.

Once she knew the prognosis, she was glad he'd moved away before their relationship had progressed any further. It spared her the anguish of confessing that she was no longer a whole woman.

Since then not even her hobbies interested her. Perhaps a little dog she could train from puppyhood would help bring her out of this depression. Much as she hated to admit, that's what it was.

If she was really being honest with herself, she'd chosen to work in Tooele because it was only eight miles from Grantsville where her family lived. For someone who'd always been so cheerful and independent, she hated it that her inability to have children had changed her into some kind of emotional cripple.

She needed to go back to Salt Lake which was far enough away that she couldn't just pop in on her parents when she felt down. If getting a dog didn't help, then she would probably have to seek some counseling.

Her mother had urged her to look on the bright side. One day when she married, she could adopt. Intellectually Meg knew her mom was right. But most men wanted to father their own flesh and blood.

It took a special man to deal with a woman's infertility. He had to love you so much he could look past the medical problem. If there was a man out there who could do that, she hadn't met him yet.

As for the tiny infant in the ICU, she could steal him away tonight and love him forever.

The fact that she would even entertain the thought proved she needed to do something about her situation as soon as possible.

A half hour later Mrs. Pope's IV had run out. "How's the headache now?"

"It's gone. My husband should be here any minute to take me home."

"I'm glad you're feeling better. Your color has come back." Meg removed the needle and bandaged the spot. "I'll tell the doctor. While I'm at it, is there anything else I can do for you?"

"Nothing. But thank you for sitting with me and being so nice. My husband has a hard time when I get like this."

"If he's good to you otherwise, I forgive him."

Her patient's wan smile told Meg all she needed to know. "He is."

Lucky you.

She went out to the desk. "Dr. Parker? Mrs. Pope's waiting to be discharged."

He nodded. "Get the lab over here, then join me in cubicle four. We've got a victim with a knife wound who's about to go to surgery."

"I'll call them."

Between that injury and a heart attack victim brought in by an ambulance, the doctors and staff were run off their feet for the next couple of hours. Around four it was Meg's turn to check on the baby.

To her surprise, Mr. Broderick was still in the Infant ICU watching the baby.

"At last," came the deep voice as soon as he saw her.

"Things got busy out there."

He rose to his full height. "So I noticed."

While she checked on the drip and various monitors, she felt his anxious gaze on her face. "What do you think?"

She knew what he wanted to hear, but she still couldn't tell him. "H-he's not any worse."

"*Damn,*" he bit out, then threw his head back. "I'm sorry."

"Don't apologize. I was on the brink of saying something unprofessional myself. He's so precious and so utterly helpless." Her voice quavered.

Lines darkened his face. "I'm afraid to leave for fear he'll—"

"I know," she broke in before he could finish. "Why don't I have a cot brought in so you can lie down next to him."

By his expression she could tell her suggestion had shocked him. "You would do that?"

"If I had realized you were still here, I would have suggested it earlier. There's no one else to keep the baby company. Finders, keepers," she said with a smile. "In the meantime, wash your hands in the sink over there. Here's a pair of sterile gloves for you. When you've dried off, put them on. Then you can reach inside the crib and touch him while you talk to him. I bet he'd like to hear how you sing, too."

She leaned close to the holes. "You haven't been on this earth very long, have you, sweetie. And every new little guy deserves all the love and attention he can get. I would say this big guy here who saved your life is the perfect person to do that. Now I'll leave you two to get better acquainted.''

Meg didn't know what had possessed her just now, but she'd sensed Mr. Broderick needed somewhere to go with his feelings. Giving him a job would help the agonizing hours pass faster.

Besides, she was a firm believer in touching babies as much and as often as possible. The ER didn't have enough staff to lavish the kind of physical love normally extended by the adoring parents of a newborn.

"Hey, Meg?" Julie signaled to her from the desk. Things had quieted down for the moment. No doubt she was going to brag about the date she'd wangled out of Mr. Broderick. Meg didn't want to hear it.

"Just a minute and let me call housekeeping first." When she'd rung for a cot to be sent to the Infant ICU, she gave Julie her attention. "What were you going to say?"

"I was hoping you would tell me," she whispered.

Meg frowned. "What do you mean?"

"I got nowhere with that guy. I mean *nowhere*. He only asked one question that didn't have to do with the baby. When were *you* going to come back in the room.''

To Meg's consternation her heart turned over.

"He probably thought I had news from the doctor. Don't forget the man found the baby. I think he's still in shock.''

"That's for sure. What a grouch.''

"The police haven't cleared him yet, Julie.''

"Oh for heaven's sake— If that were the case, he would never have brought the baby in!''

"I agree it's absurd.''

"Uh-oh. We've got a new customer."

Meg looked over her shoulder in time to see the paramedics come through the doors pushing a gurney. An old tramp lay there bundled in a blanket. He looked half dead. The poor thing probably hadn't been able to find shelter from the storm. She wished she were immune to sights like that, but it hadn't happened yet.

Zane could hear someone screaming.

"Johnny? I'm coming! Hang on!"

The screaming grew louder, bringing Zane fully awake from an old nightmare. He'd broken out in a cold sweat and his heart was pounding like a locomotive.

It took him a second to remember where he was.

He rubbed his eyes and raised up on the cot to get a better look at the wall clock. It was almost noon!

The last time he recalled anything, it was Ms. Richins who'd come in to check on the baby.

The baby!

Zane's heart skidded to a stop before he levered himself from the cot, terrified he would find the crib empty.

Relief flooded his system to see the infant lying in the same position as before. Without hesitation he put on a new pair of gloves, then fit his hands through the holes of the crib.

When he put out his finger and brushed it against the baby's left hand, the little guy's fingers responded and clung to him the same way they'd done last night.

A lump lodged in Zane's throat. "I told you to hang in there for me, and you did."

With his other hand he smoothed the fine dark hair

on the tiny head. He studied each perfect feature, the shell ears, the minute finger and toenails. There weren't any lashes yet, but his eyes looked like they might be open a tiny slit. Surely that had to be a good sign!

"Dear God, if you aren't a miracle!"

A middle-aged nurse he didn't recognize came into the room. She smiled when she saw him standing at the crib. "Sorry if the noise woke you. I heard you were here all night and figured you needed the sleep."

"I should have been up before now. What does the doctor say about the baby's condition today?"

"At this stage, things are tentative."

His spirits plummeted. He should have known better than to ask. "Do you have any idea what time Ms. Richins will be on duty again?"

"She works the night shift. If she's scheduled for tonight, she'll be in at eight p.m. Is there anything I can do for you?"

"No, thank you. I wanted to let her know I appreciated the cot."

"She went home at five-thirty this morning, but I'll pass your gratitude along."

"Thank you."

He touched the baby's flailing hands once more, then pulled his own hands out of the crib.

"I'll be back later," he whispered. "Get better for me now."

After tossing the gloves in the waste bin, he reached for his cowboy hat. Before walking out the door, he hesitated.

"There is one thing," he said to the nurse. "I carry a cell phone. If there's any change in the baby either way, could someone phone me immediately?"

"Of course. Write your number at the top of the chart hanging on the front of the crib."

He walked back and put it there with an attached pencil, but once that was accomplished, it was almost impossible to walk away from the baby. Zane felt like he was leaving a part of his heart.

"Babies are stronger than you think." The nurse could read his mind.

"I pray you're right."

When he stepped outside the ER, the sunlight nearly blinded him. One thing about Utah blizzards. After they'd blown themselves out, the bluest sky on earth magically appeared.

At least a foot and a half of wet, heavy snow, maybe more, had blanketed the world around him. Its whiteness dazzled the eyes. He had his work cut out to clear it off his truck before he could see enough to drive home.

After snow-blowing his driveway and the front path leading to the porch, he went in the house and checked his answering machine. The police hadn't called, of course.

Still full of anger, he headed for a hot shower. In case his cell phone rang, he kept it on the tile sink so he could hear it.

Later, when he'd put on a clean shirt and jeans, he rustled up some food for a sandwich, but his stores were low. He needed to do something about that before the guys pulled in tonight.

First, however, he needed to talk to his crew, then straighten the house. He had a cleaning lady who came in once a week, but there were still things to do.

Three hours later he took off for the supermarket and loaded up on supplies. On his way down one of the aisles looking for napkins, he found himself stopping in front of the disposable diaper section, something he'd never done before in his life.

There were several brands for newborns. Zane felt a pit in his gut when he thought of Johnny struggling for life beneath the heater of his crib.

As his gaze strayed to the baby bottles, pictures of the tubes and IVs hooked up to those five precious pounds of humanity flooded his mind, bringing tears to his eyes.

He blinked them back before heading to one of the checkout counters. Once he'd put the groceries away, he'd drive out to the ER and stay with Johnny. When the guys phoned, he'd give them directions to the hospital so they could see the baby before they all moved on to his house.

Hopefully Ms. Richins was working tonight and would come on duty while he was still there. For some reason the image of her gleaming brown hair and eyes like rich, warm drops of melted chocolate, managed to intrude whenever he thought about Johnny. He couldn't seem to separate the two in his mind.

There was a sweetness in her voice and expression around the baby. Zane had been charmed by her.

When Meg went out to her car at seven p.m., she told herself it was because she needed time to scrape the ice off her windshield so she wouldn't be late for work. On a clear night after a storm, everything froze.

But the job only took five minutes, and her Jeep could go anywhere in the snow without problem.

When she walked into the ER at seven-twenty, Dr. Parker's head turned in her direction. She'd forgotten his hours were different than those of the staff.

He checked his watch. "You're forty minutes early tonight. In case you're looking for Baby Doe, he's not here."

"*No!*" she cried in agony, and started shaking her head.

"Take it easy, Meg. I meant that it was *good* news. He's still sick, but stabilized. I took him off the extremely Critical List and had him transferred to the nursery around dinnertime."

"Thank heaven!" She clung to the counter, still trying to recover.

"I guess we should have hung a sign. When Mr. Broderick discovered the baby wasn't here, he reacted the exact same way you did."

"He's here?" Just the mention of the stranger's name brought this suffocating feeling to her chest.

"Obviously he *was.*"

Without conscious thought Meg raced around the corner and down the hall. She opened the door and took the stairs to the nursery one floor up.

"Where have you put Baby Doe?" she asked Shelby Clark, one of the nurses at the station.

"You mean, our little celebrity? I'm afraid you'll have to stand in line outside the sick baby nursery," she teased. "At the moment there are three people ahead of you. They're all men, and they're gorgeous!" she confided.

"If *you're* up here, that means the word has already spread to the main floor. I think every eligible female in this hospital is waiting her turn for a glimpse of them. Donna says they're movie stars here on location for a film."

Donna was wrong.

The men were probably the engineers helping Zane

Broderick on his project. But Meg kept those thoughts to herself.

"I just want a peek at the baby before I go on duty in a few minutes."

"Sure you do." Shelby winked.

Under other circumstances Meg would have enjoyed Shelby's innocent teasing. But not tonight. Meg was too close to this case. Dr. Parker had upset her too much.

If she'd found Dr. Tingey in the ER, his first words would have been, "I have good news. Baby Doe has been transferred to the nursery."

But that wasn't Dr. Parker's style. Telling her the baby was gone had almost given her a heart attack. Aside from her other reason for leaving Tooele, the thought of not working around Dr. Parker any longer than necessary held a lot of appeal.

It was just as well she'd talked to Debbie this morning about moving back to Salt Lake. To her surprise, her roommate admitted she'd been worried about Meg and thought a change of scene sounded like a good plan for her.

Meg also learned that Debbie had been considering moving home to Logan, Utah, where she could stay with her folks and attend graduate school at Utah State. But she'd been hesitant to talk to Meg about it because she didn't want to leave her in the lurch.

Not only had their talk helped Meg decide to give two weeks' notice to the hospital, Meg's first reaction when she heard the baby was gone proved her emotions were too involved to be healthy.

Hard as it was to do, she decided it would be better not to see the baby again. Now that he'd been moved to the nursery, there was no reason for Meg to be up here. No reason at all.

This was the crucial moment to practice self-restraint. Otherwise she would be in a much worse condition when child welfare services came to the hospital.

The police report was already in their files. Any day now, probably as early as tomorrow, a social worker would show up to find out how soon the baby could be placed in foster care.

Already the abandoned infant had endeared himself to Meg. Because of Mr. Broderick, she no longer thought of him as Baby Doe. In her heart, he'd become Johnny.

She needed to make the break while she still could. It meant she wouldn't be seeing Mr. Broderick again, either. He made up the other part of her forbidden list.

"You know what, Shelby? I think I'll come back when there isn't a line. See you later."

Meg left the floor, not interested in remaining there to catch up on hospital gossip. Once she'd reached the ER and had hung up her coat, she plunged into her work with a vengeance.

If there wasn't anything going on between crises, she took inventory of supplies in the cubicles, anything to keep so busy she wouldn't think about what was going on upstairs.

"What's with you?" Julie asked when there was a quiet moment. Meg had been counting boxes of gloves and syringes. Her colleague's question threw her off.

"Just trying to make myself useful."

"Well stop it! You're putting me to shame."

Meg was still down on her haunches. "Sorry, I hadn't realized."

"Hey— I was only teasing. What's wrong? You don't seem yourself."

"Let me get you something for it."

"I took some tablets while I was hanging up my coat, but thanks anyway."

"Sure. Did you know Baby Doe was transferred to the nursery?"

"Yes, I heard. I-it's wonderful."

"Lucky, too."

"What do you mean?"

"The police were here a few minutes ago looking for that gorgeous grouch who brought the baby in. At least now they can't pin a murder charge on him."

Upon that revelation, Meg dropped the clipboard. After grabbing for it, she got to her feet. "Surely they weren't here to arrest him!"

"I don't know. Dr. Parker sent them to the nursery."

Adrenaline surged through Meg's body. "Julie— It's quiet right now. Would you cover for me? I'll be back inside of ten minutes."

"Of course. You spelled me off last night when I missed all the action. Give me the clipboard."

"Thanks."

She dashed out of the cubicle and ran down two corridors in search of the stairs. Once she'd reached the next floor, she headed straight for the sick baby nursery.

Through the glass of one of the partitioned rooms, she could see Zane Broderick talking to the policemen who'd come to the ER last night. Two other men as tall and attractive as he was stood close by, their expressions equally solemn.

If those officers were reading him his rights…

Heedless of the consequences, Meg marched into the nursery, swept past the staff and opened the door where Mr. Broderick was being interrogated. All eyes swerved in her direction.

"Excuse me for interrupting," she began, "but if you're still thinking this man had any knowledge of Baby Doe's situation prior to his finding the baby and bringing him to the ER, then you're way off base, gentlemen.

"He's the engineer who built that track where the baby was found. If he'd had anything to hide, he would never have admitted to finding the child *there* of all places."

She struggled for breath. "I was here all night to observe him. He never went home. In fact I had to get him a cot because he was dead on his feet, but that didn't matter to him. He hovered over that baby, talked to it, touched it— He *willed* it to live, officers.

"I haven't seen most fathers show that kind of love or concern or devotion for their own offspring, let alone for a nameless baby someone had left out to die!"

By now she was trembling. "Why don't you gentlemen get out there and beat the bushes to find the birthparents of that adorable little baby? You'll probably discover it was a couple of terrified fifteen-year-olds who don't have a clue about the sanctity of life!

"I'm telling you right now that if you charge this man with the crime, I'll fight you every step of the way. When you hear what Dr. Tingey, the head of the ER, and one of the most powerful figures in this community, has to say about this matter, he'll make mincemeat of you in court!"

Silence filled the room.

"Are you quite through?" one of the officers inquired in such a mild-mannered voice she wanted to scratch his eyes out.

"For now." She was still bristling with rage.

His eyes held a mysterious twinkle. "That's good, because we came to bring Mr. Broderick his jacket and let him know he's no longer under suspicion. For one thing, his blood type isn't the same as the blood type on the blanket.

"For another, fresh horse manure droppings along with the bloody droplets matching that on the blanket, were found in the snow at the end of the track where Mr. Broderick rescued the infant from certain death.

"We're now looking for someone who rode a horse to that spot. Someone who couldn't have ridden very far considering the baby had been born within the same hour of his being placed there.

"Don't worry, Ms. Richins. We've been beating the bushes for the last twenty-four hours. Hopefully we'll discover the person who did this and learn the identity of the mother before too much more time passes.

"Your breathtaking defense of Mr. Broderick has been duly noted and will go in the record." He cocked his head. "If I'm ever in need of someone to stand up for me, I'll know exactly where to come.

"Goodnight, Ms. Richins. Gentlemen." He nodded to the others before he and his partner left the room. The door closed behind them with a click.

Meg wasn't a person who blushed easily. But she felt heat sweep up her body into her face and hair.

Talk about resembling a red light globe—

The two dark-haired men stood there openly smiling down at her with their eyes as well as their mouths.

She didn't dare look at Mr. Broderick, but she could feel his intense gaze scrutinizing her.

"Ms. Richins." He broke the silence with his deep voice. "I'd like to introduce you to my best friends, Dominic Giraud and Alik Jarman."

They shook hands with her.

"It's a pleasure to meet you," said the one with the French accent.

"I wouldn't have missed this," the other man teased gently. "We flew out from Denver to offer our support."

Denver? She'd thought these men were part of his crew!

"But obviously none was needed," the Frenchman added silkily.

She tried looking anywhere else, but ended up meeting Zane Broderick's penetrating regard. He wasn't smiling.

"If the officers had come here to arrest me," he began in a husky voice, "I'm not sure they would have carried out their objective after hearing your testimonial."

He folded his arms. "You risked having to pay a fine, or worse, for harassing a police officer in the line of duty. A mere thank-you for your sacrifice doesn't quite cover what you did for me just now."

"I would have done it for anyone I felt was innocent," she defended, hoping lightning wouldn't strike her for that particular white lie. "I'm very glad you're no longer under suspicion."

His eyes darkened to an inky blue. "So am I. But until the baby is completely out of the woods, it's a little too soon for the celebration I have in mind."

Her heart wouldn't stop hammering.

"He *is* improved though. Otherwise Dr. Parker wouldn't have upgraded his condition. We can be thankful for that much."

"I'm thankful you were there when the baby needed you most."

The fervency in his tone caused her to avert her eyes. "Then we're both thankful, because you're the one who found him in time." Feeling out of breath, she backed away from him. "If you will excuse me, I'm supposed to be on duty in the ER. I-it was very nice meeting all of you."

Needing to be strong right now, she purposely refused to look at the baby as she hurried through the nursery. Midway across the room, Shelby stopped her flight.

"Wait up! I found out who those men in the other room really are. Donna was wrong about them being movie stars."

"I know. They're Mr. Broderick's friends from Denver."

"They're a lot more than that!"

"I'd like to hear it, but I've got to get back to the ER."

"I'll walk you to the door. Get this— Dr. Silvano recognized them from a television appearance. The three of them are these fabulously weal—"

"Shelby?" Meg interrupted. "You'll have to tell me later. Otherwise I won't have a job."

For many reasons, including a decent recommendation when she left the clinic in two weeks, Meg needed to get out of there and back to her own floor.

CHAPTER THREE

"ARE there any more barbecued ribs?"

"Sorry, Dom. We ate all seven pounds of them."

Dominic shook his head. "You know something, *mon ami?* You missed your calling as a master chef."

"Coming from an exacting connoisseur, that's a real compliment."

"It's true, Zane," Alik concurred. "Blaire's a great cook, but nobody does ribs and baked beans like you."

"Since you guys flew through sleet and storm to bail me out, I thought the least I could do was make it worth your while."

"I'd say a certain beautiful nurse already did that." Dominic grinned.

Alik grinned back. "Here I was feeling sorry for you having to be stuck out here in the back of beyond. How long have you been holding out on us, you sly old fox?"

Zane pulled the warm, store-bought blueberry pie from the oven and set it on the table with a pitcher of cream.

"I swear I never saw her before last night."

Dominic served everyone a large piece. "It appears the *ravissante* Jeanne D'Arc is very much alive."

A chuckle escaped Alik. "Did you see the fire in her eyes? She was amazing! Those police officers are never going to forget it."

"None of us will," Dominic murmured.

Reaching for the pitcher, Zane poured cream over his pie. "She's crazy about the baby. I know for a fact she would have championed anyone who'd found him."

"He's an awfully cute little tyke. It's hard for me to believe our baby was ever that small," Alik said.

Dominic swallowed another bite. "Hannah's going to be giving birth to our child next year. Looking at that baby tonight made me realize all the things that can go wrong. I confess I'm getting nervous."

Zane studied his friend. Dominic had two vulnerable spots. His wife and adopted daughter, Elizabeth. "Your baby is going to be born in a hospital with the best medical care there is. The situations aren't comparable."

"He's right, Dom," Alik cut in. "But since I didn't know about Nicky until after he was born, I can only imagine the fears you must experience once in a while.

"Speaking of fears—" Alik eyed Zane. "Dom and I are aware of your concern for the baby. Why don't you go over to the hospital and check on him while we clean up? When you get back, we'll talk about the test run."

"I don't have to go."

"Yes, you do," Dominic insisted. "All evening we've sensed your preoccupation."

"I'm sorry. I didn't know it was that obvious."

Alik frowned. "Don't apologize. We understand. Once you've ascertained he's holding his own, you'll be able to think about something else."

"That's the problem. He's going to be sick for a while."

"All the more reason to reassure yourself he's okay tonight."

They understood him too well. "You're right. I'll leave now and be home before you know it."

Five minutes later Zane pulled into the parking lot of the hospital. Though he hadn't expected to remain under police suspicion too much longer, it was a relief to walk through the main entrance knowing they'd crossed him off their list.

There were three babies in the sick nursery. Two sets of exhausted-looking parents who'd been in there earlier were still doting on their offspring.

When Zane's gaze flicked to the other side of the semidark room and fell on one lone crib, it felt like a giant hand had just squeezed out his heart's blood. He rushed over to the baby.

"I'm here, Johnny. I'm here."

He threw off his jacket and helped himself to a pair of gloves from a nearby cart. Snagging a rolling stool with his boot, he planted himself at the side of the crib.

"I came as soon as I could." Carefully he put his hands through the holes and caught the baby's tiny fingers. They curled around his with astonishing strength and his little legs kicked harder.

"It looks like you've missed me, too." The thought that the baby recognized him thrilled him to the core of his being. "Remember those men you met? They're home doing the dishes so I could come and be with you.

"No man ever had better friends. I'll bring them over tomorrow so the three of you can get well acquainted. You'd like that, wouldn't you?"

He molded his palm to the baby's chest. "It's warm and snug in there, but I bet it's boring."

As if the baby understood, he suddenly yawned, endearing himself to Zane that much more.

An hour passed before he was even aware of it. When he happened to look up and saw that it was after eleven, he realized that if he didn't leave now, the guys would probably turn in.

"I have to go, Johnny, but I'll come back in the morning." It was a wrench to tear himself away. "Be a good boy and get well for me while I'm gone."

After discarding the gloves, he grabbed his jacket. With a nod for the nurse on duty, he exited the room only to collide with a woman intent on entering the nursery.

His hands automatically went out to steady her. She must have washed her hair with some kind of peach shampoo. The scent was intoxicating.

"I'm sorry!" she cried. "It's my fault for bumping into you."

When she lifted her head, he discovered it was Ms. Richins who'd been in too big a hurry to watch where she was going. Since he'd planned to talk to her in the ER before going out to the parking lot, nothing could have pleased him more.

He stared into her dark-fringed eyes, fascinated by their velvety brown color. "I'm glad you did. I think little Johnny's lonely for company."

After a pause, "I'm still on duty in the ER, but thought I'd dash up here for a minute and check on him. Does he seem improved to you?"

Considering she was a nurse, her hopeful question was one for the books. But from the moment he'd met her, he'd also been aware that she was a warm, caring woman. Evidently he wasn't the only person who'd fallen under the baby's spell.

"It's probably my imagination, but I thought he was a little more active tonight."

"That's a good sign."

"Is it?" His heart lurched.

"I'll know better when I look at him."

"Let's do it together."

She lowered her eyes. "I thought you were leaving."

He wasn't sure how to take her remark. "Actually I was on my way downstairs to talk to you about his condition."

By tacit agreement they entered the nursery. She made a beeline for the crib.

"Hello, little sweetheart." She tapped a knuckle against the transparent top. "What have you been doing tonight?"

At the sound of her voice, Zane noticed how Johnny turned his head toward her. His arms and legs wiggled. Anyone watching her smile at the baby could be forgiven for thinking she was the mother.

"My goodness—you *are* more animated! That's wonderful! I wish I could stay with you."

Zane knew exactly how she felt.

"Keep fighting, sweetheart."

"Hi," a female voice spoke behind them. Zane turned his head. It was one of the other mothers. She was alone and looked washed-out. Apparently her husband had left. "The waiting gets hard, doesn't it."

"Very," Zane murmured.

"You two surely have a cute baby there. He looks perfect. Sam and I were wondering what was wrong with him?"

In the next instant Ms. Richins had backed away

from the crib. Maybe it was a trick of light, but he thought there was more color in her face than before.

"H-he's not ours," she stammered. "Unfortunately I don't have time to explain because I'm due back in the ER. But I'm sure Mr. Broderick will be happy to answer your questions. I hope your baby gets well very soon. Goodnight."

Damn.

She'd gotten away from him before he was ready to let her go. Worse, she'd put him in a position where it would be rude if he didn't stay to talk to the young mother for a moment.

Without going into any details, he gave the woman a brief account, then excused himself by explaining that he had friends waiting. As he left the nursery, she was still shaking her head in disbelief.

By the time he reached his truck, he'd determined to drive over here again at five-thirty a.m. In six hours Ms. Richins would be off duty. If Johnny's birth-mother wasn't found and no one came to claim him, Zane had the burning need to know what was going to happen to the little guy...

Meg put on her parka, ready to go home. It had been an exhausting shift. She wasn't scheduled to work again until Monday night. That meant she could enjoy three days of relaxation before she needed to come near the hospital.

Three days you're not going to see Johnny.

She shouldn't have gone up to the nursery last night. But during a lull in the ER, Dr. Tingey had asked her to bring him back a progress report on Baby Doe. Social services needed the information.

Just hearing the dreaded words made Meg shudder.

Forgetting her promise to stay away from the baby, she'd rushed to do the doctor's bidding. To her humiliation, she'd run into Mr. Broderick.

Six hours had passed, yet she could still feel his strong grasp on her arms, the imprint of his hard-muscled frame against her body. The contact had sent a yielding feeling of delight through her system.

There'd been other men in her life. *This one was different.* She'd sensed it the second he'd come running into the ER clutching the baby.

In her heart of hearts, she knew instinctively this was *the* man for her.

But even if a miracle happened and he felt an attraction, she could never be *the* woman. Not with her medical history. Not to a man who clearly loved children as much as he did.

There was nothing for it but to stay as far away from him as possible.

If the hospital could find another ER nurse to replace her before her next shift, maybe she could walk away this weekend and not look back.

Tomorrow she would call Dr. Tingey at home. When she told him her reasons for quitting, he would talk to the head of personnel to help speed up the process.

As she left the ER through the emergency entrance, she heard her name called. At the sound of that vibrant male voice, her body quickened.

Not three feet behind her stood a clean-shaven Zane Broderick. She noted he was wearing a brown leather bomber jacket. Tan Levi's molded his powerful thighs. When she lifted her gaze to his burnished face once more, his blue eyes seemed to be charged with a new brilliance.

He looked so…while she looked so…

It wasn't fair!

"Good morning. I'm glad I caught you before you left the hospital."

Her heart did a wild kick. "You were waiting for me?"

"Yes. I'd like to talk to you, but not here. After an all-night shift in the ER, I realize the only thing you want to do is go home to bed. This won't take very long. Have breakfast with me at Ruth's Diner. It's only two blocks from here."

You go with him now and you'll be making a fatal mistake.

"I'm sorry, but I can't spare the time. Someone's waiting for me."

There was a perceptible hardening of his strong jaw. "Then we'll talk while I walk you to your car."

Meg hadn't expected that.

"All right," she said in a shaky voice. Biting the underside of her lip, she started through the sliding-glass doors to the parking lot. It had been plowed, but this early in the morning, before the sun made an appearance, the frigid air covered everything in a thick film of ice.

He put a hand on her elbow to assist her. Another jolt of electricity coursed through her body.

Why had he appeared at the precise moment she'd made up her mind to do something about an intolerable situation?

"Have you heard anything from the police about Johnny's mother?"

"No."

Ice cracked beneath their feet as they approached her Jeep.

"When I got home last night, my friends told me the story made the ten o'clock news."

"I knew it was only a matter of time."

"In this obscure hamlet, you would think someone who knew she was close to full term would question why she's no longer pregnant and has no baby to show for it!"

He sounded as angry as she felt.

"I know. Perhaps if the networks carry the story for a few more days, someone will come forward. A grandparent, or a sibling."

She heard his sharp intake of breath. "And if no one does?" The question hung in the arctic air like a live wire. "That's what I wanted to talk to you about."

It hadn't taken him long to get down to the crux of her pain.

She opened the Jeep and climbed inside. In the process of helping her, the brush of his hand on her hip produced another shock wave, turning her bones to liquid.

Once she'd started the motor, she rolled down the window of her hardtop.

"Then the state office of child and family services will take custody of him and place him in temporary foster care."

A frown marred his handsome features. "How soon do you think that might happen, provided no one claims him?"

Her eyes closed tightly for a moment. "As soon as he's well enough to leave the hospital."

"Which isn't going to be for some time."

She knew what he was thinking, because she was thinking the same thing. But it was no good wanting to prolong the inevitable. Certainly not at that darling baby's expense.

"They've already called Dr. Tingey. A case worker from the state office here in Tooele is coming to the hospital on Monday to open a file on the baby."

"That fast?" he bit out.

"Only the Internal Revenue Service wanting their money works faster. Ironic, isn't it, that a mother would literally discard her baby without compunction when, in fact, it's the state's number-one priority to find the mother of the abandoned child and restore it if possible?"

She was on the verge of losing complete control. "I—I'm sorry, but I have to go."

Jamming the car in reverse, she backed away from the snowbank and drove off. Before she could get the window rolled up, great heaving sobs shook her body. Something was out of balance in a world where a baby was left on a train track to die, and she couldn't even keep one of her ovaries.

Euphoric over the successful Sunday test run following another heavy snowfall on Saturday night, Zane was glad his friends' quick trip to Tooele had been worth the trouble. The train had achieved a speed of 430 miles per hour, the highest to date.

One of these days soon he would get the speed up to 500. At that rate, passengers could travel in luxury on a cushion of air from New York to San Francisco and still be able to enjoy the scenery.

After the hundreds of frustrations, problems and in some cases, agonizing setbacks, they were beginning to see daylight on a project that had captured their imaginations ages ago.

If it weren't for a tiny baby fighting for his life in a nearby hospital, Zane would have gone back to Laramie with Alik and Dominic. As it was, the three of them agreed it would be best to postpone the celebration until he knew the little guy was going to be okay.

Now that Monday had come around and they'd left for the Salt Lake airport, he could stay at the hospital with Johnny and wait for Ms. Richins to come on duty without having to worry about anything else.

The nurse in the sick baby nursery spoke up the minute she saw him enter the room. "I was expecting you this morning, Mr. Broderick. There's been a development."

He froze.

Had one of the baby's relatives shown up?

Instead of being happy for Johnny, he felt this sinking sensation in the pit of his stomach.

"Look over there."

He turned his head. The baby was *gone*. His body broke out in a cold sweat.

Zane wheeled around in panic. "Where is he?"

The nurse seemed startled by his reaction. "This morning he was taken off the critical list and put in the well nursery down the hall. I knew you would be pleased with the news."

"*I am,*" he said after he'd recovered from his fright.

Experiencing something beyond euphoria, he hurried out the door to the other nursery.

"Where have you put Baby Doe?" he asked the first nurse he saw.

She smiled. "I'm holding him."

What?

"You're the man who saved his life, aren't you?"

He nodded.

"Why don't you wash your hands and put on a gown. Then *you* can take over my job while I see to the other babies."

Two minutes later she placed a weightless bundle in his arms. "If he starts to cry, I'll show you how to feed him."

With a trembling hand Zane removed the edge of the sterile hospital blanket and gazed down in wonder at the perfect little boy dressed in a white nightie with mittens. All the tubes had been taken away. His cheeks looked fuller. His skin had color.

Zane could scarcely credit this was the same dying infant he'd rescued from the track.

A surge of emotion welled up inside him. *"Johnny,"* he whispered in a husky voice, too choked up to talk.

The tiny lids opened to reveal eyes of a nondescript hazel color. They stared up at him in quiet absorption, but Zane had heard from Blaire, who'd recently given birth to Alik's son, that newborns couldn't really see yet.

"I'm here, little guy, and I'm not going anywhere."

The baby's mouth formed a perfect O.

You do know me.

In that instant, he felt a bond with the baby so strong and tangible, it stunned him.

"Here." The nurse came by and put a cloth over his left shoulder. "Put him right up against you. Let him nestle his head under your chin. Newborns like to feel another heartbeat. It soothes them, gives them security."

Zane needed no urging.

"Make sure one of your hands is supporting his

head and neck. Otherwise he'll flop around like a rag doll.''

Dear Lord. The baby's warmth and utter sweetness brought out feelings in Zane he didn't know were there. Johnny felt so right in his arms. He smelled so good.

For the next hour Zane hugged the baby to him. He guessed Johnny was hungry when he made noises and started moving his head as if he were looking for something.

After giving him another kiss, he spoke to the nurse closest to him. ''I think he's ready to eat now.''

''That's good.'' She prepared a bottle and brought it over to him. ''There are three ounces of formula in here. Let's see how much he'll take.''

Zane settled him back in the crook of his arm, then reached for the bottle. By now Johnny had worked himself up into a good cry. Zane couldn't help but chuckle.

''Insert the nipple firmly and he'll grab on. When he's drunk an ounce, you can burp him to get rid of any air he swallowed, then give him some more.''

This was Zane's first experience handling a baby, let alone feeding one. He'd never even thought about what was involved.

When he felt the strong tug, a smile broke out on his face. ''You like that, don't you, Johnny.''

The baby drank steadily and made a funny noise with each swallow. The whole time his eyes stayed focused on Zane. Before he remembered to burp him, Johnny had drunk the whole three ounces.

Nervous he'd made a mistake, he raised the baby to his shoulder. No sooner had he settled him than a burp resounded. It was loud enough that the nurse heard it.

She laughed. "Sounds like he enjoyed himself. How much did he drink?"

"All of it," Zane admitted with a sheepish grin.

She walked over to rub the baby's head. "Do you want to know a secret? The nurse on the morning shift couldn't get him to take the bottle. Then you walk in, and he acts like he's been doing this forever."

Inexplicably touched by those words, Zane cuddled the baby closer beneath his chin.

"We may have to hire you to take care of him until he's released from the hospital. What are you doing for the rest of this week?"

She was teasing of course, but terror seized his heart. "I take it social services have been here."

"Yes. The case worker came this morning. By the weekend the baby will have finished his regimen of antibiotics. Then he'll be leaving us, won't you, young man." She rubbed his head once more, then went on about her duties.

Zane stayed to give Johnny his next feeding and received a lesson in how to change his diaper. By then it was almost five-thirty p.m. As soon as the baby fell asleep on his shoulder, Zane laid him down in the crib and covered him with the blanket.

"Sleep well, little guy," he said with a kiss to his cheek. "I'll see you later."

"Leaving so soon?" The nurse's eyes twinkled. "If you get here tomorrow morning around nine, that's when we bathe the babies. I'll show you how to do it."

He imagined Johnny would love his bath. "Thanks for everything."

"Thank *you*. Babies need all the love and attention we can give them. When we get one in here who doesn't have any visitors, we're grateful for people like you.''

Her words haunted him. "Does that happen very often?''

"More than we like to see. I'm not talking about abandoned babies. I'm talking about women who give birth here, but for one reason or another don't want much to do with their child. Some mothers don't seem to have a strong nurturing instinct. In many cases there is no father around.''

"That must be hard on all of you.''

"True, but we're compensated by taking care of sweet little souls who've just come from heaven.''

That was Johnny.

He found it difficult to swallow and could only nod to the nurse before he left the nursery.

His next destination was the ER. Before Ms. Richins went on duty, they needed to talk. He'd been anticipating their meeting all weekend and felt rather breathless as he walked through the double doors of the emergency room. Things seemed fairly calm.

The blond nurse who'd let him know she would like to get better acquainted, lit up when she saw him.

"Hi!''

"Hello, Ms. Becker. Has Ms. Richins come on duty?''

Her face fell. "I haven't seen her yet. If you want to go in the lounge, I'll tell her you're here when she comes.''

"Thanks. I'd appreciate that.''

Five minutes turned into ten. Zane watched the evening news on the lounge TV, but couldn't concentrate. Every time someone came in, he expected to see her. To his surprise, he finally saw someone he recognized. It was Dr. Tingey. The older doctor walked over to him. Zane rose to his feet and the two shook hands.

"I hear you've been cleared of suspicion in the Baby Doe case."

"Yes, much to my relief. Because of you and Ms. Richins, the little guy's doing great now."

"She's the best ER nurse I ever worked with. I understand you were waiting to see her."

"That's right."

"I'm sorry. Julie had no way of knowing that Meg isn't going to be with us anymore."

Zane blinked. "You mean, she's gone to another floor?"

"No." Dr. Tingey shook his gray head. "She resigned."

Resigned? Zane felt like he'd been kicked in the gut. "I had no idea. I've got to get hold of her immediately. Do you have her home phone number?"

The older man pursed his lips. "It's against hospital policy to give out personal information. What I *can* do is get your number and ask her to call you."

"Please."

Pulling out his wallet, Zane handed the doctor one of his business cards.

"This is my cell phone number. She can reach me anytime. Tell her I don't care if she calls me in the middle of the night. It's an emergency."

The doctor nodded before they took their leave of each other.

Zane trusted the older man to contact her. It was Ms. Richins he wasn't sure of.

If he didn't hear from her by noon tomorrow, he would do whatever it took to get in touch with her, illegal or otherwise. In the meantime, he would grab a meal at the Bar-S Corral with some of the crew. They needed to hammer out a work schedule for the next week.

Later he would come back to the hospital to be with Johnny for the rest of the evening. He was betting that Ms. Richins made an appearance. Knowing how much she cared about the baby, he couldn't fathom her staying away from him, even if she had resigned.

Zane gunned the truck's accelerator.

The whole business about her no longer working for the hospital sounded suspect to him. Her decision to leave had to have been extremely sudden. Too sudden, or Ms. Becker would have known about it.

Two nurses who worked the same shift in a place where every night was a continual life-and-death drama pretty much knew everything about each other, especially something that had to do with their job.

His hands tightened on the steering wheel. Dr. Tingey knew what was going on. He would have been the first person Ms. Richins approached about quitting.

Frustrated because her disappearance had put a wrinkle in his plans, he didn't realize he'd passed a certain brown and white Jeep leaving the Bar-S Corral until he'd slipped into a free parking space.

CHAPTER FOUR

"I DON'T know if you've noticed, but I think we're being followed by a truck. Take a look!"

Since leaving the restaurant, Meg hadn't been aware of anything except her own turmoil. Debbie's observation prompted her to glance in the sideview mirror. Sure enough a truck was gaining on her. But because it was dark out, she couldn't tell its make.

By the next stoplight it had moved behind them and had started honking. "I don't know anyone who owns a white truck. Do you, Debbie?"

"No! But they definitely want us to pull over."

"I'm not going to do it."

Meg gunned the pedal, making a sharp right turn down the next street. To her chagrin, she had to brake for a tow truck. Someone's car was being pulled out of a snowdrift from the last storm.

"We're trapped," Debbie muttered. "A tall guy in a cowboy hat just got out of his truck."

Suddenly Meg recalled the police officer asking Mr. Broderick if he owned the white Chevy V8 parked outside the emergency room.

Her heart started to run away with her. "Good grief. I—I think I know who it is."

"After the description you gave me, I do, too. He's the man who found the baby on the track. Right?"

"Yes."

With a trembling hand, Meg rolled down the window.

When he lowered his head so he could look at her, he didn't say anything for a minute. He didn't need to. His piercing gaze was eloquent with meaning.

"I—I'm sorry," she sputtered in embarrassment. "If I had known it was you, I would have stopped."

"I'm assuming this sort of thing happens to you quite often," he mocked dryly.

She felt heat prickle her face. "No."

"I have eyes in my head. Two good-looking women driving around Tooele are a natural target anytime, especially at night. I'm Zane Broderick, by the way," he said to her friend before Meg could gather her wits, let alone remember her manners.

"I'm Debbie Lignell, Meg's roommate. She told me about your heroic rescue of that little baby."

His eyes narrowed on Meg's face once more. "Hardly heroic," he came back in a sober tone. "He's the reason I followed you."

"Has Johnny taken a turn for the worse?" Meg cried out in panic.

There was a slight pause before he said, "No. Quite the opposite in fact. That's why you and I have to talk. Do you have time now?"

"We were just going back to our apartment," Debbie volunteered before Meg could stop her. "Why don't you follow us?"

This was one time when she wished Debbie weren't in her confidence. But it had been impossible for Meg to hide certain feelings about Zane Broderick from her friend. Otherwise Debbie wouldn't have understood all Meg's reasons for wanting to leave Tooele as soon as possible.

His eyes searched Meg's. "If you'd rather, Debbie can drive the Jeep and we'll follow in my truck so we can talk," he suggested smoothly. "Whatever is easiest."

"That might be the best plan, Meg. I need to do a couple of errands before the stores close."

Meg had done everything possible to avoid seeing him again. Now that he'd caught up to them, there was no escape. Standing this close to her, she could feel his warmth through the open window. It made it difficult to think, let alone breathe.

"I'll come with you." She'd tried to keep the nervous excitement out of her voice, but knew she'd failed miserably.

His eyes held a satisfied gleam before he opened the door and helped her down. With that swift male grace she admired, he went around to give Debbie a hand. As he assisted her into the driver's seat, she thanked him, then flashed Meg a private message that needed no translation.

Zane Broderick is one of a dying breed.

Meg already knew that. "See you in a little while, Debbie."

Within seconds he'd ushered Meg into his truck, and had gone around to the other side to back it up to the corner.

Debbie followed in the Jeep. They waved her off, then he turned to Meg.

"Which way to your apartment?"

"Keep going five blocks, then turn left and go six more. You'll see a small complex on the left."

"That sounds easy."

Besides the interior of his truck being surprisingly comfortable and a good deal warmer than her Jeep, their bodies weren't as close to each other as before. She was just starting to feel a little more in control of the situation when he said, "Dr. Tingey told me you resigned from the hospital. I want to know why."

Good heavens—

"And please don't insult my intelligence by telling me you suddenly developed an aversion to your working conditions, because I wouldn't believe you. Not after the praise you heaped on Dr. Tingey in front of my friends as well as the police.

"He's going to be phoning you, by the way. I told him I needed to talk to you ASAP, and gave him my cell phone number."

Her mouth had gone dry. She moistened her lips with difficulty. "I'm moving back to Salt Lake where I used to work."

He darted her a questioning glance. "That tells me your future plans, but it still doesn't explain why you didn't give two weeks' notice. Quitting cold turkey implies a problem of some kind."

"Did Dr. Tingey tell you that?" she cried out aghast.

"He didn't have to. Your co-worker, Julie, had no idea you weren't coming back to work. That pretty well told the whole tale."

She averted her face. "I don't mean to sound rude, Mr. Broderick, but what I do with my life, or why, couldn't be of any possible concern to you."

"When you hear my proposition, you'll understand why I beg to differ."

Proposition?

Meg couldn't imagine what he was getting at.

"I waited for you to come on duty in the ER so I could talk to you about it, but you never showed up. Fortunately Dr. Tingey saw me and took pity."

While she was still trying to figure out what this

conversation was leading up to, her apartment complex came into view.

"Where now?"

"You can pull up to the curb at the far end of the building."

Once that was accomplished, he kept the engine idling for heat, then turned to her.

"I spent most of the day with Johnny. The nurse showed me how to feed him a bottle and change his diaper. The little guy and I got along great."

The pictures his words conjured touched Meg's heart. She stared out her window in an attempt to fight tears without him being aware of it.

"The problem is, he's doing so well on the antibiotics, she said he'll be discharged at the end of the week. So far no one has shown up to claim him. If no one does, that means—"

"That means he'll be put with a licensed shelter family," she cut in before he could finish. "A hearing will be conducted within seventy-two hours. Then the judge will give the state custody so he can be placed in foster care. Yes. I'm well aware of the facts." Her voice trembled.

A long, tension-filled silence permeated the cab's interior.

"I've done some research," he finally spoke. "As I understand it, if I start the process of becoming a foster parent now, the state will allow me to take care of Johnny. If no relative comes forward, and I'm beginning to think that might never happen, then I plan to adopt him."

Adopt? her heart cried. "You're not serious!"

"Why not?" he fired back.

She could have swallowed her tongue. "I didn't

mean to offend you, Mr. Broderick. I—it's just that you're a single man with a demanding career and resp—''

''Exactly. I can't be home twenty-four hours a day. There are times when I have to travel, sometimes out of the country. In another month or two my work will be finished here, and I'll be making a permanent move to Laramie, Wyoming.

''What I need is someone who will live in for a temporary period to help me make a home for Johnny. You're the only person who comes to mind that I feel is eminently suited for the job.''

Meg lurched forward on the seat.

He'd lost her when he'd said he planned to adopt Johnny. She'd been sitting there in a kind of stupor. Now he wanted her to *what?*

''According to Dr. Tingey, you're the finest ER nurse he ever worked with. But as far as I'm concerned, your greatest qualification is that you love Johnny as much as I do.''

She couldn't believe what she was hearing.

''Money is no object to me. Today I was going to ask if you would consider leaving the hospital to come and work for me. But learning of your resignation has solved that particular problem.

''If you quit your job here because the salary was too low, I'll pay you a great deal more than what they're offering you in Salt Lake.

''The thought did occur to me that money might not be the culprit. Perhaps you're leaving Tooele because of an unhappy love affair. If that's the case, rest assured we'd be moving to Wyoming before too long, which would provide you with a change of scene and a chance to heal.

"Of course there's the possibility that you've decided to get married, and that's why you're moving to Salt Lake. Dr. Tingey didn't say anything about a future husband to me.

"I've given that some thought. Perhaps you and your spouse would be willing to live in Tooele for a while so you could watch Johnny for me. A lot of people commute to Salt Lake from here. I'd pay a generous salary that would compensate your husband for having to travel back and forth."

Good heavens— Mr. Broderick would go that far to enlist her help? If she needed proof that he truly loved the baby he'd rescued from the track, he'd just given it to her.

"*Are* you going to be getting married right away?" he inquired in a silky voice.

She shook her head without looking at him. "No. A man has nothing to do with my leaving Tooele or going to Salt Lake." Her voice trembled. "But even with your generous money offer, I'm afraid my answer has to be no."

"Do you have family problems then?" he asked, undaunted. "If it's a question of needing to help a sick parent or a relative, they'd be welcome at my house, too."

This was too much.

"No—" she blurted. "It's nothing like that."

"I know you're crazy about Johnny."

"I am!" she confessed before he could say another word to break her down a little more. "But that's not the problem!" she lied.

"Then what is?" Even in the semidark interior of the cab, his eyes blazed a hot blue.

The problem is *you*, Mr. Broderick. I think I've

fallen in love with you, and you only see me as a live-in nanny.

"It's inevitable Johnny would get attached to me. It would be a wrench for him when I had to leave. Cruel, in fact. He deserves to have someone around on a permanent basis, not just a month or two."

"I couldn't agree more, and I have a solution. In fact I would have suggested it in the beginning. But first I needed to find out if there was a man in your life."

"I don't understand."

"Marry me."

"Don't be absurd!" she responded with an angry laugh.

"I never saw the necessity of marrying," he went on as if she hadn't made an outburst. "But if you came to live with me for Johnny's sake, a wedding ring would make everything respectable. Behind closed doors we would continue to be employer and employee—live our own personal lives the same as before."

In other words he not only *didn't* see her as an object of his desire, he had no intention of giving up other women.

"Naturally I wouldn't expect you to make such a sacrifice without compensations. If you consent to my proposal, I'll write a check you can deposit in your personal bank account that ensures you will never have to work another day in your life if you don't want to.

"If there came a point down the road where you met someone and wanted to marry for love, we'd divorce quietly and work out visitation so Johnny would always have you in his life. The offer of money would still stand.''

''An open marriage isn't a marriage, Mr. Broderick. It's a mockery!'' she blurted, hot-faced because she was so confused and hurt and angry all at once.

''I happen to agree with you. Don't you know I only mentioned marriage to satisfy *your* sensibilities? Not mine.''

How could a man who wanted to adopt someone else's child be so cold and cynical about the man-woman relationship? It explained why he was a confirmed bachelor, but it would never make sense to her.

''Why would you be willing to go to these lengths for a baby who's not even your own flesh and blood?''

There was a brief silence. ''When I was nine years old,'' he began, ''my twin brother Johnny drowned in San Francisco Bay, leaving me an only child. We'd been out floating on rubber inner tubes not very far from shore. His suddenly deflated.

''I tried to save him, but he couldn't stay up long enough for me to get to him. I watched him go under that dark blue water. Since then, I've heard his screams every night in my sleep.'' His voice grated.

Dear God.

''My father tried to get me help by taking me to the best psychiatrists in the States and Europe, but the trauma was too horrifying and always stayed with me.

''When I found the baby half dead on the track, the unspeakable horror of that moment came flooding back. It was like *déjà vu*. He became Johnny. I had to find a way to save him.''

Now she understood the pain in his eyes when he'd come running into the ER clutching the baby. Her eyes squeezed shut for the agony he'd been forced to endure.

"Today while I was feeding Johnny, I knew in my gut he was going to be all right. The way he accepted me, the way he felt in my arms—it made me realize I can't let him go. I want to be his father. I want him to be my son."

Meg no longer questioned his attachment to Johnny. It was everything else she couldn't handle.

"It wouldn't work to marry you. Johnny would still know I was his nanny. He'd grow up without respect for the time-honored institution of marriage. That's no way to raise a child."

So saying, she opened the door and climbed out of the truck before he could help her.

Halfway to the stairs of the apartment, he caught up to her and grasped her shoulders. When he swung her around to face him, their breath mingled in the freezing night air.

"Let's get something straight, shall we?" he muttered with refined savagery. "If you become Mrs. Zane Broderick, you'll be Johnny's mother in every sense of the word."

Something in the naked intensity of his gaze caused her to believe him. His offer of marriage was legitimate.

She looked down.

To be a mother, but not a wife...

"Shall we drive over to the hospital and see him? Maybe that will help you make up your mind."

No! That would be the worst idea.

"I understand why you can't answer me," he taunted. "It's because you know that if you lay eyes on Johnny one more time, you won't be able to walk away from him anymore than I can.

"Isn't the idea of him being given up to foster care the real reason you decided to work at another hospital? So you wouldn't have to stand by and watch it happen?"

The man whose hands held her in a viselike grip understood too much about life, about her. His uncanny instincts terrified her. If she weren't careful, he would figure out the other reason she'd wanted to leave Tooele as soon as she could.

"I think you're getting ahead of yourself!" she cried before backing away from him so he would have to release her. "Johnny's birthparents are out there somewhere, and they have families. Someone's going to break the silence and step forward before the week is out. His story is in the paper and on the news day and night."

"That's right, and as I understand it, there have already been thousands of calls pouring in from people all over the country wanting to adopt him if the state gets custody."

It was true! She'd heard it on one of the cable networks before she and Debbie had gone to dinner. Meg had immediately shut off the TV in an effort to blot out the pain.

"Provided no one claims Johnny by the end of the week, I have the best chance of his being placed with me if I start attending the class for foster parents tomorrow. My intention to adopt him can only make the ultimate decision weigh in my favor.

"From what I've learned, there's not a lot to be done. They'll run a criminal background check on me, and come by the house to inspect it for a safe environment. With your help we could turn one of the guest bedrooms into a nursery and provide it with everything Johnny would need.

"The fact that you're a registered nurse isn't one of the prerequisites. But you can't tell me it wouldn't impress the case worker, especially if he or she knows you were my wife and going to be a stay-at-home mom.

"But it's your decision. If you turn me down, I'll advertise for a nanny because I'm determined to take Johnny home with me. Call me later when you've made up your mind. Here's my cell phone number."

He drew one of the business cards from his wallet and put it in the palm of her hand, curling her fingers over it.

The tension between them was palpable. "If the answer is no, would you be thinking of a woman who might want the job? The only requirement would be that she put Johnny first, and love him like a mother. If she passes that test, then I don't need to worry about the other details."

He shifted his weight, calling her attention to his hard-sinewed body. "Which apartment is yours? My apologies for keeping you out here too long," he changed the subject while she was still reeling from his unorthodox marriage proposal.

"Up the stairs on the left."

"Then I'll watch you until you're safely inside. Another minute out here and you're going to freeze to death. Call me anytime between now and six-thirty in the morning. If I don't hear from you, then I'll realize I was wrong about your feelings for Johnny and make other plans. Goodnight, Meg."

He'd never called her by her first name before.

"Goodnight," came her tremulous whisper before she darted away from him.

Needing to channel his energy with something physical, Zane went back to the hospital to give Johnny his ten o'clock feeding, then he hurried home to his tiny three-bedroom bungalow.

The smallest bedroom in the house had been used for a storeroom. There was no basement, so he moved everything to the separate garage out back which he never used. By two o'clock in the morning the room stood empty.

After washing the windows and walls, he vacuumed the carpet, then started a major housecleaning of the other guest bedroom, which already contained a double bed and dresser.

When Dominic or Alik came to Tooele, they used that room. If they were both here at the same time, the Hide-A-Bed couch in the front room served a second person perfectly well.

Around five he fixed himself some eggs and drank a quart of orange juice, all the while waiting for the damn phone to ring. When it got to be six, adrenaline made him nervy.

A shower and fresh change of clothes did nothing to improve his darkening mood.

Zane had taken a lot of risks in his life. Particularly the bullet train venture in which he'd laid everything on the line. Yet he'd always felt certain of a positive outcome, until now...

It was past six-thirty. Apparently he'd read Meg Richins wrong.

Hell.

What more could he have offered her?

In angry frustration he opened one of the kitchen cupboards and reached for the Jack Daniel's, something he only ever did by way of celebration. Never alone.

Upon pouring himself a glass, he downed the contents in one swallow. As it burned its way down his throat, he put on his jacket and cowboy hat, then strode through the house to the front door.

Once he got things squared away with the crew, he would drive over to the hospital to bathe Johnny. It was an experience he was living for despite his disappointment.

He *was* disappointed.

In fact it shocked him how upset he was that she wouldn't be the body living in the guest bedroom, taking care of Johnny.

It wouldn't be her voice talking to the baby in that special way of hers that had charmed Zane from the beginning.

To his chagrin he would have to contact a nanny service and make certain someone could be on hand by the weekend to help him with the baby until he found a permanent, live-in nanny.

In the meantime there was a great deal to accomplish before this day was out. He needed to file an application to become a foster parent and sign up for the class.

Though it was possible Johnny might end up going home with a relative, Zane had this gut feeling it wasn't going to happen. How much of that feeling had to do with wishful thinking, he couldn't tell. He only knew that he wanted Johnny in his life and wouldn't let anything stand in his way.

The newspaper boy had already been by. Zane

tossed it inside the house to read later, then slammed the front door and locked it.

To hell with Meg Richins!

Ready to jump the short flight of stairs, he came to an abrupt halt when he heard a familiar female voice call his name. He lifted his head.

It was still dark outside, but he would know her slender silhouette and long shapely legs anywhere. His pulse raced.

"Meg? What are you doing out here alone? Why didn't you phone?"

He watched her pull the lapels of her parka closer together. "Because I still haven't made a decision."

She was giving his heart the workout of its life!

"For one thing, I'd like to see the place where I'd be taking care of Johnny. You and I are virtual strangers. To be honest, I came over here to catch you off guard. Maybe that sounds horrible to you, but you can tell a lot about people by the way they live."

Zane smiled, thanking the powers that be that he'd been in the mood to do all the housework last night.

"Your caution gives further proof that you're the right person to mother Johnny. Come in and look around to your heart's content. My red-brick bungalow may be small and sparsely furnished, but until I move to Wyoming, it's adequate for my needs."

"That's another thing I want to talk to you about."

"Why don't we do that over breakfast." He unlocked the door and ushered her inside.

"I couldn't eat right now, thank you, but please go ahead if you're hungry."

"Actually, I ate a little while ago." He turned on the front-room lights. "Let me take your coat."

She had to be at least five foot seven and looked

terrific in jeans. He admired the bounce of glossy brown hair against her shoulders. He couldn't help but notice the full curves beneath her black turtleneck sweater. Until now she'd always been covered up by her parka or lab coat.

Depositing both their coats and his hat on the couch, he showed her into the kitchen. Her gaze darted around the room until it rested on the bottle of scotch still sitting on the drainboard next to the empty glass. *Damn.*

"You said you wanted to catch me," he drawled.

One corner of her mouth lifted. "That's a very nutritional breakfast."

"If I told you it was my first in many years at this time of the morning, would you believe me?"

Her warm brown eyes studied his features before they met his gaze. "Yes. I could tell you'd just had a drink before you came out on the porch. As for the bottle, it's almost full. I have to assume you were waiting for my call. It tells me you've been desperate for an answer."

This woman had hidden depths he was only beginning to discover.

"You're right," came his solemn answer. "Is Meg short for Megan?"

"Yes. Do you have a middle name?"

"Jeremy. My mother's maiden name."

She nodded. "Can I see where you plan to put Johnny?"

"Down this hall at the end. There's a bathroom between his room and the other guest bedroom you would use. My room has its own bath and is closest to the kitchen."

He showed her the entire floor, including the washer and dryer out on the back porch off the kitchen.

"You keep a cleaner, neater house than I do," she admitted when they'd come back to the living room.

The constricting bands around his chest loosened. "I have to make another confession. I was up all night getting things ready. Why don't you sit down."

She took a seat in the nearest chair and crossed one lovely limb over the other. It struck him how ultimately feminine she was in everything she said and did.

"With all the wonderful things manufactured for babies today, I have no doubt that little room would make a perfect nursery. Your house is very comfortable."

"I'm glad you approve." He hooked his leg across one of the wooden chairs and rested his chin on the back of it. "Go ahead and fire all the questions you want at me."

"Does the nature of your work require you to move often?"

"No. I've lived in Tooele the entire time I've been working on the train design. Another month and my part of the project will be finished. The move to Laramie is going to be a permanent one.

"I'll be renting a house there until the home I'm planning to have built is finished. It's on the same piece of property where Alik and Zane are building homes for their families.

"We're in business together and we'll be overseeing the bullet train project for many years to come. For obvious reasons it makes a lot of sense that we live by each other."

"Especially when they're your best friends," she interjected.

He nodded. "When Johnny's a little older, he'll be in heaven. Dominic's wife, Hannah, is expecting a baby in five months. They already have a little girl they've adopted named Elizabeth who's about a year old. As for Alik, he and Blaire have a little boy, Nicky, who's probably close to four months now."

"You'll all be new fathers together."

Zane liked the sound of that. Last week he couldn't have imagined it. He still couldn't imagine it if the woman across from him decided she couldn't bring herself to marry him.

Now that he was getting to know her a little better, he realized she wasn't the kind of person who would consent to be a live-in nanny for a bachelor.

It had to be marriage, or nothing at all.

"If leaving Tooele would be your main objection, I'd be prepared to put off the move to Laramie for several years. I would want you to feel comfortable. Does your family live here?"

"In Grantsville. My father's a mechanical engineer who works for the Tooele Army Depot. We're originally from South Dakota. When he retires, they'll be moving back to the family ranch in the northwestern part of the state, but that won't be for a while."

"What about sisters and brothers?"

"I have one of both. They're married with young children. Kathie lives in California, and Brett in Nebraska."

"That means Johnny would have cousins."

"Three of them. Two girls and a boy, all under the age of four."

"Are you the baby?"

"Yes. But I would never let my emotional ties to family interfere with a move as important as the one you'll be making to Laramie. Of course you have to be close to the men who developed this project with you!"

Suddenly she stood up.

Just when he thought they had reached some kind of understanding, he felt her pulling away from him.

"So what are you saying?" he demanding quietly, getting to his feet.

"All of these plans are premature if someone claims Johnny before Friday." She reached for her parka and slipped into it before he could help her. "W-why don't we talk again later on in the week when we know more."

He gritted his teeth. "No. For a variety of reasons, I have to have your answer now."

Even from the distance separating them he could see she was trembling.

"What if we've been married for a few days or a week, and find out we have to give up Johnny because a relative has come forward?"

"We'll cross that bridge when we come to it."

Her head flew back. "But then we'll have married for no good reason!"

"We'll have it annulled for non-consummation of our wedding vows."

CHAPTER FIVE

MEG wore her reliable navy two-piece suit with the eggshell-colored blouse to be married.

Zane had told her she could have any kind of wedding she wanted. He'd even suggested a church if that was what she preferred, but she couldn't! Theirs wasn't going to be a real marriage.

She couldn't believe she'd actually gone through with it. But when Friday morning arrived and Baby Doe was still unclaimed, the case worker signed the order that Zane could take the baby home with him as soon as the doctor released him from the hospital.

At that point, Zane called Meg and told her to get ready because they were flying to Reno, Nevada, at noon, and would return later in the day.

In the end they repeated their vows before a civil servant at the county register's office, with strangers for witnesses. The afternoon ceremony took three minutes, ending with a cool kiss from Zane on her cheek, and a combination solitaire diamond and gold band on her ring finger.

On their way back to Tooele from the Salt Lake airport, a thirty-minute drive, they stopped at the general mart for a crib and baby essentials including infant formula. They would shop at the local furniture store on Saturday for a baby dresser.

At ten p.m., after the pediatrician had made his final rounds, they took John Richins Broderick home with

78

them to the cheers of the combined nurseries' staff and Dr. Tingey.

Everything passed in a kind of blur as Zane insisted Meg give Johnny a bottle while he brought their purchases in the house and set up the baby bed.

It wasn't until she was sitting alone on the couch for a minute cuddling the tiny baby who'd fallen asleep against her shoulder, that the enormity of what she'd done assailed her.

Even if it was temporary, Johnny was her baby boy right now, hers and Zane's. The process had been done legally and aboveboard. Zane would be a fully certified foster parent by Christmas.

Christmas.

This year she would be spending it with her own husband and child, a blessing that, since her operation, she'd believed was meant for other people, not her.

Johnny darling— You fill the ache in my arms, in my heart.

Unable to contain her joy, tears ran down her cheeks.

"Everything's done." Zane came to stand next to her. "Are you all right?"

"Yes." She sniffed and dashed the tears from her face with her free hand. "Here—you put him down in his new bed. I know you've been waiting for this moment. While you do that, I'll make up the formula and put the bottles in the fridge."

He leaned over to take the sleeping baby from her, but he didn't walk away yet. "I realize this is a strange experience for you, Meg. It is for me, too, but I swear I'll do whatever it takes to make this work."

Normally intuitive, Zane had misunderstood the reason for her tears and was doing his best to help her overcome any misgivings. She could never fault his sincerity.

If she hadn't known from the very beginning what an honorable man he was deep down inside, she would never have agreed to this ménage-for-the-baby-only.

"I will, too," she assured him. "Johnny deserves to be raised in a happy home."

As soon as he disappeared, Meg headed for the kitchen. Because she'd been over on Monday and had imagined herself living here ever since, it already felt like home. All it would take was a few days to learn where he kept everything.

It didn't take long to prepare six bottles. As she was putting the last of them in the refrigerator, the phone rang. Not Zane's cell phone, but the one on the wall in the kitchen.

Afraid the ringing might disturb the baby, she reached for the receiver. "Hello?"

After a slight pause, a deep male voice said, "Is this Zane Broderick's residence?"

"Yes."

Another pause ensued. "Is he there?"

In her nervousness, she twisted the phone cord with her fingers. "Yes, but he's busy right now. Can I take a message and have him call you back?"

"Of course. You wouldn't happen to be the nurse who told off those police officers at the hospital, would you?"

Warmth crept into her cheeks. "Yes, and you must be Alik."

"How did you know?"

"Because you're the one who doesn't have a French accent."

She heard a chuckle on the other end. "I can't wait

to tell Dominic. He doesn't believe he has one any-more.''

Meg smiled. "Please don't say anything to him. It's a very slight accent, and all the more attractive because of it.''

"I take it this phone call is for me," Zane mur-mured close to her ear. She almost dropped the re-ceiver.

"Alik? Z-Zane's just came in the kitchen. Here he is.''

Averting her eyes, she handed it to him. Anxious to give him privacy, she decided to check on the baby. Before she reached the hall she heard Zane say, "We brought Johnny home tonight. By the way, Meg and I were married in Reno earlier today. That was my wife you were talking to.''

She lingered outside the door, waiting to hear him qualify that statement. When he spoke again, this time in hushed tones, she was relieved. It meant Alik now knew it was a marriage in name only.

It was fine for the rest of the world to believe they were a normal couple who'd married for love. That had been the plan. But she was glad he hadn't lied to his friend about something so fundamental. Soon Dominic would be privy to the truth. Now she wouldn't feel awkward around Zane's best friends.

If Sunday hadn't been such a beautiful winter day, Meg wouldn't have dreamed of taking Johnny out in the Jeep. But her parents didn't know anything yet. Before more time passed, she needed to tell them what she'd done before they heard it from someone else.

Meg had been up with the baby all Friday night. Because of that, Zane had insisted on getting up with him the next. Right now he was sound asleep. It was the perfect time to visit her parents who would already have been to church.

After leaving him a note on the kitchen counter where he would be sure to see it, she fastened Johnny in his new baby seat and drove him to Grantsville. On the way, she had to stop at several lights. Each time she saw other mothers driving their children around, it brought her inestimable pleasure that her own little baby was snug in the back seat.

When she entered her parent's house, she found them in the living room reading the newspaper.

"Meggie!" They both put down their papers.

"Don't tell me," her mother said. "That's the abandoned baby!"

Her father looked worried. "I didn't know the hospital would let you take him out."

"Don't worry, Dad. I didn't steal him," she teased. "Come here, sweetheart." She removed the blanket covering the infant seat and undid the straps so she could pick him up. He looked adorable in the blue quilted snowsuit Zane had bought for him yesterday.

She undid the zipper and pulled down the hood so her parents could get a really good look at him.

Her dad broke out in a broad smile. Her mother oohed and ahhed as Meg handed the baby to her.

"Oh look, John! Isn't he a perfect little treasure! With that dusting of hair, he reminds me a lot of Brett when he was born. How could any mother give you up?"

Meg's mom raised him so she could kiss his cheeks. Her dad moved next to her and patted the baby's back.

All night long Meg had pondered the best way to tell her parents what she'd done. No matter how she explained things, it would come as a tremendous shock.

By morning she'd decided to present Johnny as a fait accommpli, which he was.

They might never understand, but at least they would warm to the idea if they saw the baby first. So far her plan was working. He'd already melted their hearts.

"Mom and Dad?" she began on a shallow breath. "Meet your newest grandson, John Richins Broderick. He weighs six pounds today, and he's twenty inches long.

"Johnny? These wonderful people are your nana and papa Richins. You're going to love them as much as I do."

Enchanted by the baby, it took them a minute to digest what she'd said.

"While you're both still trying to recover, let me explain."

In the next few minutes she'd told them everything. There had never been secrets in the Richins home. She wasn't about to start now.

Her father stared at her misty-eyed. "You must have wanted to be a mother very badly to have agreed to his proposal."

"I—it's more than that, Dad. I'm in love with Zane."

"Honey—" Her mom shook her head. "You've known him scarcely more than a week!"

"I realize that. But we had to act quickly before Johnny was placed in foster care with someone else. If you could have seen Zane with the baby like I have, you would understand how much he loves him. I told you about his twin brother, how he lost him."

"But this man doesn't love *you!*" her father muttered. "He's hired you to be a round-the-clock baby tender."

The truth hurt, especially coming from her father. "I know." Her voice shook. "But you're not a woman who can't have children, Dad! There aren't very many men like you who would marry a woman knowing he couldn't father his own child.

"Until Johnny came along, Zane never planned to marry. Maybe losing his brother made him afraid of commitment. But with me, there's no emotional investment. Don't you see?"

"Except on your part, honey," her mother whispered tearfully. "Meggie—don't you see what you've done? By becoming this man's wife, you've condemned yourself to a loveless marriage."

"But I have Johnny. He's all I'll need."

"You say that now because Johnny has filled the terrible void left from your operation. But mark my words. One day you're going to want more."

"No, Mom. If you ever met Zane, you would understand why no other man could appeal to me now."

"He's not in love with you, darling. In time that's going to kill you."

"Did he actually tell you he was going to see other women on the side?" her father demanded, sounding angry.

"No, Dad. There's something you don't understand. Before the subject of marriage was broached, he asked me to be a live-in nanny."

Her parents looked stunned.

"Then why didn't you say yes to that?" her mother cried.

Meg averted her eyes. "Because it wouldn't look proper."

Her father let out a deep sigh. "You're right, Meggie. I don't understand. You mean to tell me you'd rather enter into a loveless marriage than have the world speculate about your relationship with your employer?"

"John," her mother called to him. "Meg's in love with him. Many bad mistakes in judgment are made in the name of love."

"This isn't a mistake, Mom. He's a bachelor through and through. He made it perfectly clear how things would be. Though the world will see us a married couple, we'll go on with our private lives. I took that to mean he would see another woman on occasion, but he'd be discreet.

"He told me that if down the road I met someone I wanted to marry, then we would divorce quietly. Of course that's never going to happen."

Suddenly her dad got to his feet. "I don't like it."

Her mother continued to rock the baby, looking sadder than Meg had ever seen her look in their lives.

"There are millions of married couples out there where one of the partners doesn't love the other anymore, Dad. At least in my case I know where I stand, and have no expectations. The point is, we both love Johnny and would do anything for him."

"You *did* do anything for him," her father muttered.

"So you can't be the tiniest bit glad for me?" she cried in pain. "You have no idea how happy Zane has made me by letting be a mother to Johnny.

"He's the most generous, wonderful man." Her

voice trembled. "You should see him with Johnny. No child could have a better father."

"You're not going to feel that way when you find out he's been sleeping in another woman's bed."

"I'm not saying it won't hurt, but I'll learn to live with it."

"Before this thing goes any farther, you could get an annulment."

She knew her dad was only saying these things for her own good. He still looked at her with love.

"I know. But I don't want one. I don't want to lose Zane."

"I felt the same way about you after our first date, John," her mother reminded him.

"That was different because I returned your feelings." His glance slid from his wife to Meg.

"Ah, honey. Come here to your old dad." He held out his arms and she went running into them. "Bring him over to the house one day soon so we can meet him."

"What's his favorite food and I'll cook it?" her mom asked.

Meg wiped her eyes. "I don't know yet, but I'll find out! Thank you both for accepting this like you have. I love you so much. Johnny's going to love you, too.

"Now I think we'd better go. Even though I left a note, Zane will be crushed because the baby's not there when he wakes up. He's crazy about him."

Her father started to say something, then thought the better of it. Meg could read his mind. She knew he was wishing that Zane was crazy about *her*.

Wishing for that was like wishing for peace on

earth. But she had her baby, and would pour out all the love she had to give on him.

Dear Zane— I took Johnny to meet his grandparents. Will be back soon. If you're hungry, your breakfast is in the oven. Meg.

Zane read the note over a couple of times.

After crushing it in his hand, he tossed it in the wastebasket, then reached in the oven.

The biscuits were light, the sausage wasn't overcooked, the scrambled eggs were dry, just the way he liked them.

It appeared he'd gotten himself a great cook into the bargain.

So far she hadn't done anything wrong. It went without saying she knew exactly how to take care of Johnny.

So why in the hell was he so upset this morning!

She had every right to go see her parents. In fact she'd probably chosen to take the baby while Zane was asleep so he wouldn't be disturbed.

As he was buttering his last biscuit, his cell phone rang. He hurried into the bedroom to answer it and said hello, thinking it might be Meg because she wouldn't have memorized the number of his house phone yet.

"*Eh bien, mon vieux*— How's the old married man today?"

He gripped the phone tighter. Trust Dominic to put the finger on the problem. Zane was married all right, but he didn't feel married. Of course, never having been married before, he had no idea how that was supposed to feel.

"Good. How are things there?"

Dom could be silent in a way no one else could. "What's wrong, *mom ami?*"

He grunted. "How do you do that?"

"Do what?"

"I swear you feel vibes when nobody else has a clue."

"Obviously this isn't the time to invite you and your family to Laramie. Hannah and Blaire have a party planned to celebrate your nuptials. We were thinking Tuesday or Wednesday at our apartment."

"Three families might make it a tight fitting."

"That's what ought to make it so much fun, if you follow my meaning."

Zane followed his meaning, all right. "Tell the girls I'm very touched. Let me check it out with Meg and I'll get back to you."

"You're not having second thoughts..."

"Hell no!"

"I didn't think so. I just wanted to hear the real you come out for a minute."

"I'm here." His voice grated.

"But you don't know what's hit you. I recall feeling the same way when this golden-haired angel wearing cowboy boots carried me off on her magic horse."

"Zane? We're home!"

"Dom? Sorry to interrupt, but I have to go. I'll phone you later. Thanks for calling."

"A bientôt, mon ami."

When he met them coming down the hall, they looked good enough to eat. He relieved Meg of the baby, but kept his eyes on her.

"How did it go with your parents? Is your father ready to have our marriage annulled?"

Dark color broke out beneath the roses in her cold cheeks. It had to have been difficult for her.

"Of course they were surprised, but they want what I want, and they've already fallen in love with Johnny. Naturally they're anxious to meet you. We've been invited to dinner whenever it's convenient."

"That makes another invitation for us."

"What do you mean?" She followed him into the nursery where he put the baby on the changing table to remove his snowsuit.

"I was on the phone with Dominic just now. My friends have planned a party in Laramie for next week. We're the guests of honor."

She looked flustered. "That's very nice of them, but I think it's a little soon for Johnny to be around a lot of other people."

Zane frowned. "Is there something wrong with him you haven't told me about?"

"No! Of course not." Her brown eyes looked wounded. "I just remember what Dr. Tingey told me about newborns. He said they're better off if they don't have to go out in public for the first three weeks or so. Under normal circumstances I would have asked my parents to come over here to see Johnny. But because of our situation, I—"

"Say no more," he cut in. "I understand. Dr. Tingey's advice makes a lot of sense. It's probably for the best if we stay in until Christmas. That way I won't have to miss any of the foster care classes."

She nodded. "Don't forget the hearing with the judge. We won't be able to take Johnny anywhere until the decision is handed down."

"You're right."

For the first time in his life he wasn't thinking very

clearly. It all had to do with this woman who was living under his roof. *Lord.* She was his wife! Only now was he starting to realize he had another person to consider when making decisions. And his son, of course.

"Zane? How would it be if we invite your friends to spend Christmas with us? We'll have a wedding celebration party on Christmas Eve, and enjoy all of Christmas Day together.

"We can rent a couple of cribs and put them in here. It will be a tight squeeze but we'll manage. As for the adults, they can use the two bedrooms and we'll take the living room.

"That way we can put the finishing touches on Christmas after everyone's gone to bed. We'll fight it out later who sleeps on the Hide-A-Bed and who gets the other couch."

The pictures those words conjured destroyed his bad mood as if it had never been. "You'd be willing to go to all that work when you have a new baby?"

"Of course. I need to get more acquainted with your friends before we have to move to Laramie. Their children will be Johnny's playmates. Besides, you forget. I didn't give birth to him, so I'm not exhausted from the delivery of being pregnant for nine months."

She kissed the baby's face while he finished changing his diaper. Once that was accomplished he hugged Johnny against his shoulder, relishing the scent of powder and her light, flowery fragrance which clung to the baby's skin.

"The guys and I have never spent the holidays together. I don't think there's anything we'd enjoy more. I'll call everyone tonight and invite them."

"I'm glad the idea appeals to you. Now—since I

can see I'm not going to get Johnny away from you for a while, do you mind if I run over to the apartment? There are some more of my belongings I need to pack up and bring here.''

"Go ahead. But after you've boxed everything, leave them and I'll pick them up later in the truck.''

"That won't be necessary. I was hired to be the nanny and can take care of myself.''

He stiffened. "When we took our vows, the word 'nanny' went by the wayside. You're my wife and Johnny's mother. We're going to be a team from now on, Meg. That means we'll both be stepping in to help each other all the time.

"You fixed my breakfast this morning, which was delicious by the way. I'll take care of your boxes this afternoon. If you can't see our relationship in that light, then I'm afraid this isn't going to work.''

"You're right,'' she admitted, nodding her head. "I guess it's because I haven't been married before. Normally I do everything by myself.''

Her explanation pacified him to some degree.

"Being a bachelor hasn't exactly prepared me to consider anyone else, either. But this little guy's presence changes everything.''

"We're so lucky he's ours.''

Whenever she looked at the baby, a softness entered her velvety brown eyes. As Zane stared down at her, it hit him how remarkable it was that she felt such a strong attachment to Johnny.

He could understand Blaire's love for Nicky. She'd given birth to him. Dominic's wife, Hannah had strong reasons for loving Elizabeth like her own because the baby was her niece. She'd raised her sister's child from birth.

But it was another thing altogether for Meg to take an abandoned baby to her heart and love him on sight. Zane suspected her response to Johnny was a rare occurrence, even for a woman who had a natural affection for children.

If his brother's death hadn't caused Zane to lose his faith years ago, he would probably be attributing this situation with Meg and the baby to destiny. What shocked him most was that he would even entertain the thought.

"Zane?" her voice called him back to the present. "I'm going to put a roast in the oven. It'll cook while I'm gone. When I get back we'll have dinner."

"That sounds good. Johnny and I will sit here and watch the ball game."

"I can tell you right now the Forty-Niners are going to lose." With that unexpected volley, she disappeared from the room. Unable to resist, Zane got up from the couch with the baby and followed her into the kitchen.

"You like football?"

Her half smile taunted him as she put the meat in the oven. "Why do you think I decided to choose this time to go over to the apartment? I figured I would stay in your good graces longer if I celebrate San Francisco's defeat in Debbie's presence."

"There's no way my home team is going to lose to Green Bay today."

"We'll see," she said with a mysterious gleam in her eye. "Word has it that Danny Lahtu's hamstring is better and he's back with the Packers in top form, ready to play."

Danny Lahtu was one of the best wide receivers in the NFL. "I didn't hear about that."

"His mom is a physical therapist at Oquirrh Mountains Medical Center."

"He's from Tooele?"

"Don't sound so shocked! Quite a few famous people have lived here," she defended. "But I don't remember their names at the moment."

As she climbed in her Jeep, Meg could still hear Zane's full-bodied laughter. She hadn't known he was capable of letting go like that. His unexpected reaction brought her more pleasure than the Packers' winning score over San Francisco at the end of the game.

With Debbie in Logan for the weekend, Meg had been able to turn up the volume on the TV without fear of annoying her friend who didn't like to watch sports.

After Meg had cleaned everything spotless and stacked the boxes in the living room for Zane to carry out, she took a last look around the apartment.

She couldn't remember the number of times she'd been through the same experience in preparation for her next move. But there was a significant difference with this one...

Her newest roommate happened to be the man she'd married so she could be Johnny's mother. Already the idea of ever having to move out of Zane's house—away from him or the baby—was something she had no desire to contemplate.

She entered the house with the one box she'd brought with her, and set it down by the back door. The TV in the front room was still blaring. When she went to investigate, she found Zane and Johnny dead to the world. The baby lay in his infant seat near his father who'd stretched out on the couch.

If they could sleep through the post game discussion going on, that was fine with Meg. She would listen while she finished fixing dinner.

By the time she'd started mashing the potatoes, Zane entered the kitchen. In a T-shirt and sweats, he looked too attractive by far.

"You should have wakened me when you got back. I could have set the table at least."

"Why? Sunday's are perfect days for naps. Father and son were out for the count."

A half smile broke the corner of his mouth. "Johnny's still asleep." But his smile disappeared as soon as his gaze flicked to the box by the door. "I thought we agreed you would let me bring your things from the apartment."

"We did." She poured the juice off the roast to make the gravy. "I wanted that carton. After dinner I'd like to finish up a project I've been working on."

Zane took a piece of pot roast off the platter. "Umm. That's delicious." He quickly stole another bite, exactly the way her father pilfered food before their Sunday meals. "Can I see what's inside the box, or is it private?"

"Go ahead."

Out of the periphery she watched him hunker down to investigate. Soon he was emptying the box like someone who'd come upon buried treasure. In the excitement, he forgot the world around him. Within seconds the floor was littered with all her paraphernalia.

"I didn't know you were a rock hound," he murmured.

"I make jewelry for a hobby."

"Where did you find *this?*" He held up her prize geode, the one with the deep red silica shell.

"In the Greasewood draw, south of Green River."

He examined it for a long time. "It's fantastic."

"I think so, too."

"Alik's a renowned geologist, but I bet this rivals anything he has in his collection. Wait till he sees it!"

"I've been told it's special. I've never come across a geode that contained so much amethyst. There's enough inside to make all kinds of gifts."

But Zane didn't comment because he was too busy unwrapping her two-inch dark red garnet, a smooth, rounded crystal of trapezohedral form. He rose to his feet and held it to the light.

"This is magnificent. Did it come from the same area?"

"No. About five years ago I discovered that particular garnet on Topaz mountain. I've kept it all this time because I'm not an expert at cutting yet. If I practice long enough on other gemstones I've found, maybe one day I'll feel confident enough to do something with it."

"What are you working on right now?" His eyes were alive with interest as they wandered over her face.

She put the pot roast on the table. "In that little green bag with the drawstring, you'll find some topaz I've cut on my faceting machine. I'm making a choker necklace for my sister's birthday."

He emptied the contents into his hand.

She was proud of the those twenty deep pink stones. It had taken forever to prepare them. "They're finally ready to be set in the gold chain I bought."

After scrutinizing them for a few minutes longer, he put the pouch back, then turned to her with a penetrating gaze.

"I'm looking forward to watching you work. In fact I'm in awe of your many talents, particularly your cooking. It would be criminal to let this feast grow cold. Shall we eat? I don't know about you, but I'm starving."

There was a tone in his vibrant male voice that turned Meg's legs to jelly. She needed Johnny so she wouldn't forget why she was living in this man's house. If she weren't careful, he would find out she was painfully in love with him.

"Why don't you sit down and serve us. I'm going to get the baby. He should be waking up any second now and will wonder where we are."

Please wake up, Johnny. I need you to keep me so busy I won't think about your daddy and the way he makes me feel.

CHAPTER SIX

"THE court of Tooele County hereby gives the Utah State Division of Child and Family Services custody of Baby Doe until further notice. Counsel for the State, you wished to address the court at this time?"

"Yes, Your Honor. Upon Baby Doe's discharge from the Oquirrh Mountains Medical Center, he was placed in the care of Mr. and Mrs. Zane Broderick, residing at 1017 Parkway, Tooele, Utah. The said couple are seated in the courtroom today with the baby.

"Mr. Broderick is the man who found the abandoned newborn on the verge of death. He is currently enrolled in the class to become licensed as a foster parent. His wife, Meg, is the registered nurse who helped care for the infant when he was brought in.

"She has since resigned from her job at the aforementioned medical center to be a full time mother to the baby. The Brodericks have already started procedures to formally adopt Baby Doe as their son.

"The case worker for the state in this matter wishes to inform the court that Baby Doe, whom the foster parents have named John Richins Broderick, is very fortunate indeed to have found a home with this fine couple who can give the child all the necessary physical, emotional, spiritual and financial support it needs.

"In the event that neither the birthmother or birthfather comes before this court to give adequate reason why they should be able to reclaim their child, it is the state's wish that Baby Doe be allowed to remain in the temporary foster care of Mr. and Mrs. Zane Broderick.''

"So granted. Court's adjourned." The judge pounded the gavel.

"Thank God," Zane muttered before he grabbed Meg around the shoulders and kissed her cheek. Joy had prompted his actions of course. But he could have no idea how that physical manifestation of affection had reduced her body to pulp.

To hide her feelings, she buried her face in Johnny's neck, thankful she'd been holding him when the judge had rendered his decision.

"Let's celebrate and buy us a Christmas tree. What do you say?"

"We'd love it, wouldn't we, Johnny," she answered, still not looking at Zane in case her eyes revealed everything in her heart.

"The problem is, I don't have any Christmas lights or decorations."

"Neither do I," she confessed. "I've always spent the holidays at my parents."

"Then let's make a day of it. After we get the tree set up, we'll drive to Salt Lake and buy the things we need. If we put the baby down after lunch, do you think your mother would be willing to tend him that long?"

"I was just going to suggest it, but can you take that kind of time off from work?"

"I told the crew they wouldn't be seeing me today."

Nothing could have made Meg happier. "When we get out to the truck, I'll call Mom on the cell phone and see if she can come over. But first I want to thank the case worker for helping us get custody of Johnny."

"OK."

Meg purposely didn't use the word "temporary" custody. There wasn't anything temporary about the way she or Zane felt where Johnny was concerned.

The rest of the day flew by in a flurry of activity. By the time she'd given the baby his ten o'clock bottle, the house looked like a Christmas card inside and out.

They'd created a forever atmosphere.

To her joy, Zane had loved the painted wooden ornaments from Germany as much as she did and went overboard in the shop. Besides the precious tree decorations, they now owned a tall, beautiful pyramid-styled wooden crèche scene of the nativity he'd set up on the coffee table.

Across the mantel of the fireplace lay a garland of evergreens entwined with tiny lights. At each end stood the exquisite hand-painted nutcrackers Zane had insisted on buying. They were sixteen-inch replicas of Maid Marion and Robin Hood in full winter costume of velvet, brocade and ermine.

Beneath the tree on the bright red Christmas tree skirt, Santa's elves played carols while they worked at their various jobs. Like a domino effect, one would beat on a drum, then another played the flute.

In a year's time, Johnny would be fascinated by everything. For this Christmas season the elves would enchant the Giraud's little daughter Elizabeth. According to Zane, his friends were thrilled by the invitation and looked forward to bringing their families to Tooele.

Meg was anticipating the event with a mixture of excitement and apprehension. So many guests in the house would force her and Zane to be together for three or four nights. Feeling the way she did about him, it would be difficult, if not impossible, to pretend that sleeping in the same room with the man she'd married in name only didn't affect her.

Innumerable times throughout the day he'd cupped her elbow to escort her to another shop, or to help her into the truck. The constant physical contact had set her nerve endings on fire.

Her body still pulsated from the pleasurable stimulation of his hip brushing against hers. The intensity of his gaze as he'd searched her eyes for answers to the simplest questions lingered to make chaos of her emotions.

Everything about their day together had been indelibly impressed in her mind. Each time Zane told the clerks that he and his wife wanted to see something else, she felt a savage pride and was rocked by an explosion of need that was growing out of control. At this rate she was in grave danger of revealing her love.

Their outing to Salt Lake without Johnny had been a mistake! In future she would make certain she spent as little time as possible alone with him. That was the only solution if their contrived marriage was going to work.

It *had* to work!

A year from now Zane would be living in his new house in Laramie. More than anything in the world she wanted to be there with him and Johnny. For that to happen she needed to be very careful from now on.

Instead of basking in the glow of the lighted noble fir while she waited for Zane to get back, she decided now would be the best time to put herself and the baby to bed. Tomorrow morning, after he'd left for work, she would get busy making Christmas presents. With

Zane's best friends coming, her list would be a good deal longer this year.

But it was figuring out the perfect gift for Zane that kept her tossing and turning the rest of the night.

In her restless state she would have welcomed getting up for Johnny's three o'clock feeding. To her surprise, Zane responded to the baby's cries before she could throw on a robe.

It was just as well. After her determination to avoid any unnecessary intimacy around Zane, she would be playing with fire to go in the nursery at this time of night when it wasn't necessary.

She slept on and off until seven, then got up and dressed to fix her breakfast. After putting it in the oven to keep warm, she filled the plastic tub and brought Johnny into the kitchen for his bath.

The lids of his eyes were beginning to show signs of lash growth. He stared up at her without blinking.

Unable to resist, she kissed his head and cheeks. "You're getting to be such a big boy," she said as she washed his hair and neck with the glycerin soap.

His chin quivered in that adorable way when she turned him over so she could wash his back and legs. As soon as she lowered him into the water again, he moved his arms and legs excitedly. "I think you love this as much as I do, don't you sweetheart."

"Who wouldn't crave all that attention." Zane's deep male voice turned her bones to liquid. He'd come into the kitchen and had moved next to her without her realizing it. When he reached out so the baby could grasp his finger, she could smell the soap he'd used in the shower. Meg felt herself drowning in sensation.

"Y-your breakfast is ready."

"Do you know you're spoiling me?"

"It was the least I could do for you."

Unable to bear his nearness any longer, she lifted the baby onto the counter and wrapped him up in his towel.

"He's beautiful," Zane murmured, powdering him before she put on the diaper.

"Perfect," was all she could manage to say because her heart was too full. Soon she'd dressed him in his shirt and the pale green velour suit with the feet. "There we go. Your daddy is dying to hold you."

Lifting the baby, she handed him to Zane, then walked around them to put his breakfast on the table and pour the coffee.

"Your mom's a wonderful cook, little guy. Too bad you can't eat any of her food yet." He sat down with the baby propped against his shoulder and began to consume his bacon and eggs.

She felt his gaze travel over her as she put a bottle in a saucepan to warm. "When will Johnny be able to take something else besides formula?"

"Not for quite a while yet," Meg answered. "It depends on how fast he gains weight, and how soon his bottles don't satisfy him. I'll ask the doctor. The baby's appointment is next Tuesday."

"I'll plan to go with you."

Her pulse raced. "M-maybe that's something you two ought to do by yourselves."

A slight pause ensued. "Is there a reason why the three of us can't go together?"

She whirled around with the bottle in hand, surprised at the negative tension coming from him. "No, of course not. I just know how crazy you are about him. It might be fun to take him to the doctor alone. A sort of boys' day out.''

He kissed Johnny's temple. ''We'll have plenty of time for that when he's older. Right now I think it's important he knows both parents are with him every step of the way.'' In one lithe movement he got up from the table and handed her the baby.

''I should be home around five. If I'm going to be late, I'll call you. Be a good boy for your mommy.'' He gave Johnny another kiss. As he lifted his head, his jaw disturbed her hair, sending delicious shivers to the very soles of her feet. A few seconds later he'd shrugged into his bomber jacket and was gone.

His swift exit from the house was a warning that she'd angered him. Anger was supposed to mask fear. Of what?

He'd always been so self-assured around the baby. It couldn't be because he was afraid of doing something wrong when she wasn't with him.

Maybe he feared she wasn't as devoted to Johnny as he'd assumed. Perhaps the suggestion about his going alone to the pediatrician's office with the baby made him think she was already feeling cooped up in their loveless arrangement.

Heavens, if he only knew the truth—

She took the baby into the living room and fed him on the couch where they could look at the Christmas tree.

''I love your daddy so much I ache inside, Johnny. How do I keep my secret and distance myself without upsetting him? The answer to that question will determine if this marriage works or not.''

Johnny was such a comfort, Meg ended up holding him for a good two hours. But at the end of that time she still hadn't come up with a solution. Out of necessity, she put the baby to bed so she could get the dishes done. Debbie rang while she was starting a wash.

Though her friend talked about the impending move to Logan on Saturday, she really wanted to know how the marriage was going. The second Debbie broached the subject, Meg tried to hide her turmoil. Of course it didn't work and everything came tumbling out.

When the tears subsided her friend said, "Why don't you just tell him the truth? That you fell in love with him and Johnny at the same time."

Meg ran for some tissues. "He was a confirmed bachelor before he met me, and those feelings haven't changed. If I bare my soul to him, he'll get rid of me so fast you won't believe it. I couldn't risk losing Johnny now."

"Or Zane." Debbie sighed. "I guess you're going to have to learn how to turn off your feelings for him. Maybe try treating him like your brother."

My brother...

Meg sniffed. "You've just given me an idea." In fact it was sheer genius and helped alleviate some of her pain.

"I liked my first one better. The truth is always best."

She shook her head. "Not in my case. Thanks for being there for me, Debbie. Don't forget, you're having a meal with us on Friday night."

"Of course I won't forget. I can't wait to hold the baby!"

After they clicked off, Meg moved the boxes Zane had left in the kitchen and living room to her bedroom. All but one contained more rock hound equipment and crystal samples. The other box held her nursing books and SCUBA manuals. Her diving gear was stored at her parents' house.

When that task was finished, she went back to the kitchen. An always considerate Zane had placed a list of his friends' cell phone numbers at the end of the counter.

Before she started making Christmas presents, she needed some information and decided to call Dominic Giraud. She was pleased when he picked up on the second ring.

"Zane—" he muttered without preamble. "We must be reading each other's minds. I was about to phone you. *Eh bien,* how does marriage feel today? I want the unvarnished truth, *tu comprends?*"

Good heavens. She swallowed hard, not knowing what to do. If she hung up, he would call back.

"D—Dominic? It's Meg. Zane's not here."

There was a certain stillness before he said, "I apologize, Meg. This will teach me not to make assumptions. But now that I know who it is, I'll ask you the same question. How does it feel to be a new wife and mother?"

Zane had told Meg that Dominic was a master at handling difficult situations with unparalleled finesse. She could believe it. But caught off guard, even he hadn't been able to hide certain undertones that only went to prove just how close the two men really were.

After the tension-packed episode in the kitchen before Zane left for work, she decided she'd better tell Dominic something that would make Zane feel secure.

"It's wonderful. Johnny is thriving!"

"I like that kind of news. No doubt by now Zane

has told you we've accepted your gracious Christmas invitation. It has already made my holiday."

His sincerity was palpable. She smiled. "I'm glad. We're looking forward to it, too. That's the reason I'm calling. I need to know something, but you have to promise not to tell your wife or Blaire."

He chuckled. "You have my word."

"What color are their eyes? I need an exact description."

"That's easy. Blaire's are a translucent gray with silver flecks. My wife's are a shimmery green, like Spring grass in a high-country meadow." His voice throbbed at the last. She heard so much love come out of him, her eyes misted over.

"What about your daughter's?"

"*Petite?*" He had to clear his throat. "Hers are green, too."

"Thank you, Dominic. One day you will understand why I bothered you."

"A phone call from you will always be a pleasure. I hope you know that."

"I do. Thank you again for your help. We'll see you soon."

"*A bientôt, cherie.*"

His use of French charmed her down to her toenails. She imagined that combined with his marvelous looks, Hannah Giraud must have had a heart attack the first time she met him.

That's what had happened to Meg when Zane came running into the ER. She never stood a chance against his overpowering male beauty.

Unfortunately the difference between her marital relationship and Hannah's was that Meg would be treating Zane like a brother from here on out. Thanks to

Debbie, she had a survival plan and could finally concentrate on other things, like everyone's Christmas gifts.

Within a half hour she knew exactly what she wanted to make for all the people on her list. Except Zane. His present needed to be something truly unique.

She rummaged through the last box of samples. Then she saw it. A treasure she'd found years ago fossicking with her friends.

As she raised it to the light, Meg remembered the exact spot where it had come from. Suddenly she understood the reason why she'd been saving it all this time.

The hairs lifted on the back of her neck.

It was December twenty-second. Zane had every reason to celebrate. When the guys arrived from Laramie the day after tomorrow, he would surprise them with the exciting news that the train's latest test run had achieved four hundred and eighty miles per hour.

Furthermore he'd finished his last foster parenting class, and his Christmas shopping was finally done.

Johnny's pediatrician said the baby was in excellent health and gaining weight. As for Meg, she kept a spotless house and was the perfect mother and cook. When it came down to it, he'd never known anyone as charming or considerate. She showed a flattering interest in the maglev project.

In retrospect he never dreamed their relationship would work out this well, or that he would have such a supportive helpmate.

Self-motivated, busy with her own pursuits, he could find no fault with her. In ways she was too good to be true, but that wasn't fair to say because she'd never disappointed him.

Intent on his thoughts, he didn't notice the sleek black BMW in front of the house until he'd parked the truck in the driveway. It didn't belong to anyone he knew. Someone was visiting, but who?

As he entered the back door with his packages, he could hear laughter coming from the living room. The intimate kind between a man and woman who had a history together. What the devil?

Dropping everything, he walked into the other room. At the sight of a well-dressed man in his late thirties seated on the couch next to Meg with one arm slung about her shoulders, something twisted in Zane's gut.

The stranger looked up from the baby who was lying on the top of Meg's legs and smiled. "Hi." Not acting the least uncomfortable, he rose to his feet. "So you're the guy who found Baby Doe. That was quite a story. Congratulations on a happy outcome. I'm Jonah Ryder, by the way."

Zane was forced to shake the hand the other man had extended. "I'm Zane Broderick," he spoke up before Meg could make the introductions. "Sorry, but I don't recall my wife telling me about you," he muttered, his gaze flicking to her.

Still playing with Johnny's feet, she behaved as if it was the most natural thing in the world to be sitting there with another man. One, moreover, who was familiar with her in a way Zane hadn't witnessed before.

He was still reeling from the shock when she said, "Jonah's a tax attorney in Salt Lake. We met in a scuba diving class about three years ago and have buddied each other ever since."

There was too much to absorb at once. "You're certified?"

"Yes."

"She's good, too!" Jonah inserted. "I have an opportunity to fly to the Cayman Islands for New Year's and wanted her to go with me. Little did I realize that since the last time we were together, she got married and acquired a baby."

Zane noticed that the other man didn't say, "husband."

He had no idea how much Meg had revealed concerning the true facts of their marriage. Naturally she had every right to tell this jerk whatever she damn well pleased.

"Are you sure I can't talk you into doing one dive with me before I leave?"

"I'm sorry, Jonah." Shifting the baby to her shoulder, she got to her feet and started for the front door. "But thank you for your generous offer, anyway. Why don't you call Neptune Divers? It seems to me that Randy's still working there. I know he would kill for a trip like that."

"No thanks. He takes too many risks."

"There has to be someone. Good luck hunting, and Happy New Year. If you make it to the Caymans, send me a postcard so I can drool."

"You're on." They kissed each other's cheeks before he turned to Zane who hadn't moved from the center of the room. "Nice to have met you."

Zane nodded, but for the life of him he couldn't extend himself more than that.

When she'd seen him out the door, she headed for Zane wearing a jade pullover sweater he hadn't seen before. She had to pull it down over the womanly flare of her hip. With her dark hair and eyes, a subtle flush on her cheeks, she looked stunning. He wondered how long this had been going on.

"Johnny and I are glad you're home." Her voice was filled with warmth. But then it always was. *Damn.* "He's been waiting for his favorite person to come. If you'll take him, I'll fix you something to eat."

He reached for the baby who smelled of her shampoo. She must have just washed her hair. The rich brown strands gleamed with natural red and gold highlights. It made Zane want to plunge his hands into all that luxurious silk.

Judging by her tousled look, the other man had been enjoying that pleasure along with a great deal more.

He sucked in his breath. "I'm not hungry, but our son *is.*"

"I've got his bottle warming. Would you like some coffee and gingerbread? I fixed it for Jonah. There's plenty left."

"No thanks."

"Did you get all your shopping done?"

"Yes." He followed her into the kitchen. "How come you never told me you were a diver?"

She went to the sink where she'd put the bottle in the saucepan. "The subject never came up."

"If you want to go, I'll take the time off and stay home with the baby."

"I appreciate that, but Johnny's my priority from here on out."

She wiped the water off the plastic and handed it to Zane. He was painfully aware of how careful she was not to let their fingers touch. It set off his anger even more, causing the baby to make an avid search for the nipple before he could drink.

"Do you still care for him?" Zane blurted. He wanted to know the truth. *Now.*

"Jonah? Heavens no. Not in the way you mean. He was married when we met. The dive master made buddy assignments and we were put together. Jonah's a very careful person, and I trust him not to panic under the water. He feels the same way about me.

"After the class was over we continued to dive together. Later he got a divorce, but he was still emotionally involved with his ex-wife when we went to the Caymans the first time. I wouldn't be surprised if they get back together one day."

He'd been trying to read between the lines. If she was lying, then she was doing a good job of it.

"Is there anything I can do for you before I turn in?"

Like a litany Meg asked that question every night, then hurried off to her bedroom where she disappeared until morning. She was always polite, friendly, thoughtful. Tonight it bothered the hell out of him.

He put the bottle on the table. The baby needed a burp. "Where do you usually dive?"

Her brown eyes looked up at him in pained surprise. "Why do you want to know?"

"Why do I get the idea you're purposely avoiding talking about it?" Pictures of her being involved with another diver in a romantic setting like the Caymans blackened his already foul mood.

She moistened her lips nervously. The motion drew his attention to the enticing curve of her mouth. "Because I don't want to hurt you."

He brows furrowed. "I don't follow."

"E-ever since you told me about your brother's accident, I haven't wanted to bring up anything that would remind you of it.''

Lord.

Her explanation had been the last thing on his mind. The truth humbled him to the point he was slow to respond.

"Do you hate the water?'' she asked in a gentle tone. "I think I would if the same experience had happened to me.''

He shook his head. "No. My father made certain I got therapy. If anything, the reverse is true.''

Her expression softened. "I'm glad. When Johnny's old enough to start swimming lessons, he'll want you to teach him.''

"I'm looking forward to that experience, but it's a way off yet. What if I learned to dive? Then *we* could be buddies.''

Silence filled the room.

"You really want to?'' She sounded incredulous. As he studied her reaction, he thought her face might have lost a little of its color. Something was wrong. It brought out his aggressive instincts.

"I always intended to learn. Where do you dive around here?''

"At Blue Lake near Wendover.''

Zane nodded. "Alik mentioned something about it. Aren't there hot pots below?''

"Yes. It's fun to dive there in the winter when the sky is blue. The water is seventy degrees and you can see fifty feet. If you reach the bottom, it's a hot eighty. But there won't be time for you to take the classes if we're moving to Laramie next month.''

She couldn't get off the subject fast enough.

Perversely, he said, "I'm sure there's at least one diving school there. We'll have to look into it."

"Do your friends dive?" She wrapped up the gingerbread and put it away.

"No."

"Maybe they'll want to take lessons with you."

So you won't have to get close to me?

"I doubt it. We do live our own lives."

Her head reared back. "Of course you do. I didn't mean anything by that. It's just that I've seen families dive together so they can take interesting trips. Since the three of you are so close, I was thinking how enjoyable it would be if everyone got certified."

"You mean Hannah and Blaire, too?"

"Yes."

Zane needed time to come to grips with his emotions which had undergone a total upheaval in a matter of seconds. He put Johnny's empty bottle on the counter.

"It's an idea worth broaching after everyone gets here."

"Oh—speaking of our guests, do you think they'd enjoy a visit from Mr. and Mrs. Claus on Christmas Eve?" There was a hint of pleading in her eyes. "My parents always dress up for the neighborhood kids. I realize Elizabeth will be too young to know what's going on, but still..."

With that revelation Zane understood the happy world Meg had come from. She would create that same happiness for Johnny. Every human should be so lucky...

"As far as I'm concerned, their visit will make Christmas." He'd finally had an opportunity to meet her parents on the day he and Meg had gone shopping in Salt Lake. It was obvious they adored Johnny. Zane was more than happy that they'd been so cordial to him. Especially when they would have had every right to exhibit their distrust.

"Really?" She broke into a full-bodied smile that took his breath.

"We're all little kids at heart, even if some of us have forgotten."

A fine mist glared her dark-fringed eyes. "Christmas has probably been a painful time for you."

"Not this year."

For once she didn't rush away. "Forgive me if I'm getting too personal, Zane, but what about your parents? They must miss you horribly. How are they going to spend the holidays?"

"Mother never recovered from Johnny's death. My father always takes her on a trip over Christmas. This year they're in Mexico City."

She searched his eyes once more. "Do they know you got married, that you're planning to adopt Johnny?"

"No."

A nervous hand went to her throat. "When do you plan to tell them?"

"I don't."

If he'd struck her, she couldn't have looked more aghast.

"Why?" she whispered.

"They blame me for Johnny's death. Naturally they never said the words. They didn't have to. Mother became a self-imposed invalid. My father bent over backwards pretending that he held me guiltless."

"It was an accident!" she cried out.

"Yes. But it was my idea to go inner tubing that

day, against my parents' express rules. In fact every adventurous thing Johnny and I did together was something I thought up. In their eyes I don't deserve fulfillment after robbing them of theirs.''

''But that's monstrous!''

''It's water under the bridge. Literally. Now that you know, we won't have to speak of it again.''

She lifted a hand to his jaw. It was the first time she'd ever willingly touched him. ''Johnny's the luckiest little boy in the world to have you for his father. Goodnight, Zane.''

Long after she'd kissed the baby and left the kitchen, Zane still stood there electrified by her touch. Tonight she'd reached out to comfort him. But he discovered that he wanted more from her than that.

Much more.

CHAPTER SEVEN

"'TWAS the night before Christmas and all through the house, not a creature was stirring..., except my wife.''

Zane was awake!

Meg let out a soft gasp. She'd been trying to be so careful while she hung all the stockings from the fireplace mantel. No matter how much time she'd allowed herself to get things ready, there were still one or two items she'd had to see about after everyone had gone to bed.

"It's three in the morning, Meg. At this rate you'll be too exhausted to enjoy tomorrow.''

He'd been asleep, causing his voice to sound deeper than normal. The low male tones permeated her body, filling her with inexplicable excitement.

"I'm almost through,'' she whispered, not daring to look at him. In the firelight, he looked like the dark-blond Adonis Julie had called him at the hospital.

It had been a mistake to touch him the other night, but his strong jawline had been too great a temptation. She'd wanted to clasp his face with both hands and kiss away the hurt until he started kissing her back as if his life depended on it. Just thinking about being in his arms produced a groan she was forced to stifle.

"This place looks like fairyland. I'm in my own home and don't even recognize it.''

His remark couldn't have thrilled her more. "That's the idea.''

"You do realize we're wall-to-wall gifts. No one will be able to get in here in the morning."

It wasn't a criticism. He sounded happy. Really happy.

After the private things he'd divulged to her about his family the other night, there didn't seem to be enough she could do to help him forget the sorrow in his life.

If she could have one wish, it would be to make this Christmas unforgettable. Of course having his best friends here went a long way to accomplishing that.

But there was a certain magic in the glow of the Christmas tree lights that had transformed the living room. The visit from Mr. and Mrs. Claus, the carols they'd sung, Zane's reading from the Bible, all those memories still hung fresh in the air. Combined with the pungent smell of pine and cinnamon-scented candles, she felt the whole house had become enchanted.

As long as Zane was awake, this seemed the perfect time to give him his gift. Once she'd decided what to make for him, she'd been consumed by it. Now that it was done, she found she didn't want to wait a second longer. Depending on his reaction, she felt it was better if they didn't have an audience.

"There's just one more thing I have to do, then I promise I'll go to bed."

He'd been lying on his side in the Hide-A-Bed watching her. At her approach, he looked startled and raised himself up on one elbow.

"This has been burning a hole in my pocket all night." She pulled the small wrapped box from her robe and handed it to him along with a card. "Merry Christmas."

He flung the covers aside and sat all the way up.

As soon as she saw his magnificent physique revealed by his T-shirt and sweats, she could hardly breathe. In the next instant she darted past the coffee table to the other couch and crept underneath the blanket.

To her surprise, he got up from the bed and stole into the kitchen. She hoped he liked it.

Dear Zane:

Years ago when I was out riding, I found two crystals which the experts told me were incredibly rare. Not only because of their size, but their color. Little did I realize that I'd stumbled across a new and fascinating hobby.

At the time, I didn't understand the significance of my find but incredibly the track covering the ground where you found Johnny happens to run through that very spot. So many coincidences have led me to believe the area is hallowed.

It only seems fitting that you and your friends, who've planned your bullet train along this route enjoy these stones.

They're a brilliant red variety of beryl. I was able to make four rings out of them. Alik's and Dominic's are set in Utah silver. Yours and Johnny's are in Utah gold.

Of course he's too little to wear his yet. But when he's old enough, it will be fun to give it to him and tell him the true story of how he was found along this route by his remarkable father.

You are remarkable, you know. I've watched you go from bachelor to loving father in a matter of minutes without missing a heartbeat. What's really astounding is that you've done it while using your genius to develop a maglev train that outrivals any-

thing the world has seen before now.
Your son has huge footsteps to follow.

Merry Christmas
Meg

Zane could find no words to express his feelings.

Struggling for breath, he opened the velvet box. Inside were two chunky gold men's rings, each with a large, fiery-red stone in the center.

With an unsteady hand he picked one up and held it to the light, marveling at the intensity of the color. That's when he caught sight of an inscription on the inner band. "Tooele."

He reached for the other ring. The words "San Francisco" were inscribed. His eyes closed tightly.

"Meg." He cried her name in a husky whisper, squeezing both rings in his palms.

The way he was feeling right now, he couldn't take the risk of going in to her until he was able to get his emotions under some semblance of control.

"Are you all right, *mon vieux?*"

Zane wheeled around, unaware that Dominic had come in the kitchen. He was carrying his daughter Elizabeth who had tears on her flushed cheeks and was hugging him for dear life.

"I'm afraid she woke up disoriented, and disturbed Johnny. Meg's in with him now." One dark brow quirked. "It's a good thing Alik and Blaire decided to keep Nicky in their room tonight. Otherwise—"

"Otherwise we'd all end up in here?" Alik finished the sentence for him. Dom grinned at their other nocturnal visitor. "While Blaire is still asleep, I thought I'd come and see what all the excitement was about."

"I wish I knew," Dominic muttered, staring pointedly at Zane.

"Here." He handed him the Christmas card. Dom held it away from Elizabeth so both men could read it.

When they eventually lifted their heads, Zane gave each of them a ring to examine. Their total silence said it all.

"Oh!" Meg cried in surprise when she walked in on the frozen tableau. She was carrying Johnny who had worked himself up into a hungry cry. Avoiding Zane's eyes, she slipped straight past everyone to the fridge for a bottle.

Galvanized into action, Zane reached for the saucepan and turned on the hot water. When she brought it to him, he trapped her and the baby against the sink. Uncaring of her reaction, he kissed the side of her neck where her skin smelled the sweetest.

"Wait until we're alone and you'll find out how much I love my gift."

By the time he let her go, her face had gone a rosy color. While she put the bottle in the water, the guys handed Zane back the rings they'd been holding.

Because of the wedding band on his left hand, Zane slid the one Meg had made for him on his right. The fit couldn't have been more perfect.

Alik turned to Meg. "I want *my* ring."

"We don't feel like waiting until the sun comes up," Dominic chimed in.

With a chuckle, she cuddled their fussy baby closer. "You guys are incorrigible. Go ahead and get them. They're inside your stockings hanging from the mantel."

Dom returned to the kitchen first and let Elizabeth

help him undo the wrapping. Alik followed a second later. Everyone took turns looking at the stones through the light from the ceiling.

Zane thought the silver setting was as stunning as the gold. "Laramie" and "New York" had been engraved inside their bands for the final touch. Soon all three men sported rings.

"I'd say this calls for a toast." Dominic uncorked a bottle of French champagne from his family's private cellar in Vence. He poured everyone a glass. "Not yet, *petite*," he admonished his daughter gently when she would have grabbed his drink.

"To *la belle* Meg, whose vision was part of our own had we but known everything from the beginning. *Salut*."

Everyone drank, then Alik proposed another toast to Meg. "From one rock hound to another, may I congratulate you on a find so rare, I've never seen beryl to equal it, let alone such fine artisanship.

"But fabulous as this treasure is, more congratulations go to Zane who spotted another kind of treasure in this back-of-beyond and brought her into the family."

Zane could tell all the talk was embarrassing Meg. But he was determined she wouldn't get away, and caught her around the waist. He couldn't remember ever being this happy.

While she fed their starving infant, he raised his glass. "To my wife—who has made it possible for me to be a father to our son—" He paused to clear his throat. "And has brought the joy of Christmas into our home."

"Here, here!"

"What's going on?"

*   *   *

Meg had never been so thankful for an interruption. The appearance of Blaire and a pregnant Hannah stumbling into the kitchen looking bewildered, helped divert the attention away from her.

As their husbands immediately plied them with kisses and champagne, Zane pulled her and the baby closer. This couldn't be allowed to go on! So far he'd been putting on the perfect performance of wedded bliss in front of his friends.

He was behaving like…like a husband in love.

If she hadn't known his behavior was for his friends' benefit, his comment about getting her alone to thank her sounded heartstoppingly real. The whole point of her giving all three of them rings was to show that she supported their great venture without making Zane's gift seem too personal.

"Since we're up, and the festivities have begun," he said suavely, "I suggest we move to the living room where more treasure awaits us. My wife has worked day and night on everyone's gifts, but she's kept everything a secret. I must admit I can't wait any longer to see what she's made for the girls."

There were plenty of heartwarming oohs and ahhs as Blaire and Hannah opened the contents of their stockings. Dominic's dark gaze flashed Meg a private message of gratitude as his wife lifted the peridot necklace and earrings from the box.

"How beautiful! You even made a matching bracelet for Elizabeth!" Hannah glowed in delight before running across the room to hug Meg.

"These are gorgeous!" Blaire cried when she lifted her topaz necklace and earrings for everyone to see.

Alik shook his head incredulously. "They're the exact color of your eyes, darling."

"I've never seen more beautiful workmanship. Thank you!" She left her husband's side to show Meg her appreciation.

"If we never make a dime off our train venture," Alik spoke directly to Meg with a twinkle in his eyes, "at least we know someone in the family who can earn money for us." A swell of voices agreed with him.

Suddenly Johnny was plucked out of her arms and Zane handed her his present. "I think it's time you opened this."

With trembling hands she undid the wrapping and discovered a Camcorder. How did he know?

She lifted her head. The blue of his eyes seemed to dazzle her this morning. "Thank you, Zane. You couldn't have given me anything I wanted more. Now we'll be able to record memories Johnny will treasure when he's older."

"That's the idea. It's loaded. I'll show you how it works."

Within a few minutes she got her first pictures of Zane holding the baby. Then the rest of the gift-giving began. They continued to open presents until the sun streamed in through the windows.

The room ended up in shambles, but as Hannah stated, Elizabeth was in heaven. She much preferred to toddle around among the papers and boxes than play with the toys she'd received.

Throughout it all, Meg captured everything on film, including little Nicky still asleep in his crib in the bedroom. But more often than not she returned to focus in on Zane's interactions with the others during moments when she hoped he wouldn't notice.

Of course he would find out what she'd been up to

when they looked at the video later. But at least she had the excuse that he was holding Johnny.

Much to everyone's amusement she eventually discovered Dominic filming her as she moved around getting shots. He ended up insisting that she sit by Zane and hold Johnny so he could preserve the moment for his own family's viewing enjoyment.

"*Eh bien, mon ami.* A kiss for posterity would be in order about now, *n'est-ce pas?*"

Faster than she could comprehend, Zane's mouth fell upon hers. She expected it to be a token brush of his lips. To her shock, it was a man's kiss, hot with desire.

She'd been dreaming of a moment like this for so long, her body experienced a literal explosion of need. Caught off guard, she couldn't prevent her mouth from opening to the increasing pressure of his.

The world receded as the urgency of his demand engulfed her in fire. She'd kissed other men with enjoyment, but no man had ever managed to evoke the kind of passionate response that made her forget who she was—where she was—

It wasn't until the noises Elizabeth was making impinged on her consciousness that she realized someone else was in the room. Then it all came rushing back to her.

She tore her lips from Zane's, horrified to discover that everyone's eyes were upon them.

"*Merci* for your cooperation." Dominic's deep voice reminded her he'd caught her response on film.

Breaking into her brightest smile she quipped, "Since my husband decided to play it up for the camera, I thought I would do the same. Now, if you would be so kind as to put our son to bed, I'll get the turkey in the oven.''

With a prayer that her remark had dispelled any fears Zane might have entertained about her falling in love with him, she handed Johnny to the man who'd just changed her world for all time.

In future she would make certain there were no more mindless moments of ecstasy, or he wouldn't be left in any doubt.

Blaire rose to her feet at the same time as Meg. ''I can hear Nicky starting to fuss. As soon as I feed him, I'll help you.''

''I have to get dressed, then I'll join you,'' Hannah chimed in, sweeping Elizabeth off the carpet before she could put another bow in her mouth and choke.

''Dom and I will clean up in here.''

Hot-faced, Meg hurried into the kitchen, needing a few moments alone to recover. But the power of his kiss was still upon her. She felt so weak, she had to clutch the oven door for support.

A strong pair of male hands unexpectedly grasped her waist from behind, forcing an involuntary gasp from her throat. ''I'm not going to apologize for what happened out there,'' Zane whispered against her ear and cheek. ''It's something we've both been craving for a long time.''

His honesty took her breath.

''But one stolen kiss isn't going to satisfy either of us. I find that I want you in my arms, in my bed, every night. That was never the case with either of my fiancées.''

Fiancées?

She groaned inwardly. ''I—I had no idea you'd been engaged before.''

"They pressed for it, but in the end I had to walk away before I did real damage."

But now that you have Johnny, you're not walking anywhere, and I'm a convenient outlet for your needs. Is that what you're saying? her heart cried in anguish.

While he buried his face in her hair, his hands molded her hips and stomach. "Much as I love my friends, I'm looking forward to being alone with you after they leave. When I take you to bed for the first time, I want us to have total privacy."

"Ooops. I'll come back later."

"It's all right, Blaire." He spoke in a calm voice, relinquishing his hold on Meg. "Fortunately for us, we have our whole life ahead of us."

"If you girls need something, the guys and I will be out back in the shed chopping more firewood. It's supposed to get down to minus five tonight."

When he left for the living room, Meg shivered. But it wasn't because he'd mentioned the plunging temperature. She was remembering a certain conversation with her parents.

"Meggie—don't you see what you've done? By becoming this man's wife, you've condemned yourself to a loveless marriage."

"But I have Johnny. He's all I need."

"You say that now because Johnny has filled the terrible void left from your operation. But mark my words. One day you're going to want more."

Meg *did* want more. She wanted Zane's love, but the word never passed his lips.

After what had happened on the couch a few minutes ago, Zane knew her desire for him was so great, she could deny him nothing.

If she refused to sleep with him, he would demand

to know the reason why. That would put her on the
same par with his former fiancées who'd pressured
him for an avowal of love he hadn't been able to give.

He still couldn't, never mind that he'd given Meg
his name and a son.

How odd that she'd dreamed about becoming his
wife in every sense of the word. Yet now that he'd
told her he wanted a real marriage, something beautiful had gone out of the fairy tale.

That was the problem.

By asking her to share his bed, the fairy tale had
become agonizing reality.

"I'm sorry if I interrupted something important."

Meg forced a smile. "You didn't."

Blaire eyed her with compassion. "For two people
who are still on their honeymoon, you've taken on too
much too soon by inviting us here. Everyone has been
aware Zane would prefer to have you all to himself."

If Meg understood her correctly, it meant Zane
hadn't told his friends the truth after all. They believed
he'd married her for love.

She shook her head. "As he said, we have the rest
of our lives to be alone. I—I wouldn't have missed
this Christmas for anything in the world."

"To be honest, neither would I." Blaire's voice
trembled. "Alik and Zane are both pretty much es-
tranged from their parents. So is Dominic from his
father.

"Since it was going to be a first for all us, Hannah
and I were both concerned how to help our husbands
enjoy this holiday. Then you extended your invitation.

"I have to tell you—the second we walked in this
house yesterday, we felt the spirit of Christmas seep
into our hearts."

Meg had felt its magic since the judge had granted them custody of Johnny.

"As for those beautiful rings, they're the symbolic fruition of a dream that others said was impossible. Every time they look down at their hands, our husbands will see your precious gift and feel a renewed sense of accomplishment and brotherhood."

"Thanks for those kind words."

"They're the truth! We married very unordinary men." Her voice cracked. "One day their names will be in all the history books."

Meg nodded. "The moment Zane came running into the ER with Johnny, I knew there was something about him that set him apart from other men."

"Alik said the same thing about you, Meg."

"What do you mean?"

"He and Dominic told us how you stood up to the police for Zane. After meeting you, I can understand why he fell so hard."

You have it all wrong, Blaire. *So wrong.*

"Believe me when I tell you—none of us can wait until you move to Laramie next month."

"If you keep this up, you're going to make me cry," Meg admitted before hugging her. "Excuse me for a minute while I shower and get dressed."

"I have a better idea. Take a nap while Johnny's asleep. I happen to know you didn't go to bed last night. Hannah and I will get the rest of the dinner started."

With the dishes done and the babies in bed until their nocturnal feedings, Zane urged everyone to gather around the kitchen table. The guys had brought the architect's drawings with them. He particularly wanted

Meg to see where they would be living, and get her input.

As far as he was concerned, the second his friends left for Laramie, his marriage to Meg was going to begin the way it should have done in the first place. It didn't matter how hard she tried to pretend she wasn't aware of him right now, because he knew differently.

The way she'd kissed him back this morning was all the proof he'd needed that the same fire burned inside her. Armed with that knowledge, he was able to sit back and enjoy the rest of the evening while he showed her the layout of Hannah's land.

"This is the train station and track on the northern border, demarcated by the river.

"Our homes will be above the bluff overlooking the river. See these three sites that have been roughed in? Ours is the one furthest west.

"The stable and museum are here on the southern-most boundary."

"We're having the whole placed fenced, and there will be a gate at the entrance," Hannah explained. "We've decided to name it the Sandhill Ranch."

"That was the name given the Pony Express way station by Hannah's great-grandparents," Zane said in an aside to his wife. He slid his hand to her neck beneath her hair where he felt warm, throbbing flesh.

Dom placed another huge sheet on the table. "What do you think?"

Zane watched Meg study the architect's renderings for Dominic's and Alik's new homes. The lines maintained the integrity of two different-looking, spacious ranch-style houses that fit into the Wyoming landscape, yet incorporated modern touches.

What she was looking at was such a far cry from Dom's ancestral home in Provence, or Alik's family mansion on Long Island, it made Zane realize how totally love had transformed their lives.

"They're perfect," she murmured in a wistful voice.

He caressed her earlobe and felt her tremble in response. "When we move, we'll work with the architect for the kind of house we want."

"I have to admit I'm excited. Until I was sixteen, I was raised on a ranch in South Dakota, and had my own horse. I've really missed it."

"You're kidding!" Hannah cried with excitement. "What breed?"

Everyone else looked stunned by the revelation, but no one more than Zane. His wife was so full of delightful surprises, he had a hard time tamping down his emotions. After squeezing her shoulder, he removed his hand, no longer daring to touch her.

"American quarter horse."

"So's mine. It's a chestnut mare named Cinnamon."

"I had a red roan we called Lollipop."

"Did you ever do any trick riding?"

"Some. I was in the 4-H Club. We performed a few stunts for our local rodeo, but it was kind of pathetic."

"Oh, boy. Wait until the girls in the Paintbrush Brigade hear about you!"

Hannah was off and running as she explained about the group of fifty women who rode together for pleasure, and sometimes to help in a crisis.

"That settles it! I'm going to take a lot more lessons so I can ride with you two," Blaire chimed in.

The guys flashed Zane secret smiles.

He slid his arm along the back of Meg's chair. "I guess the first thing we're going to do when we move to Laramie is get you a horse."

"I can't imagine anything more wonderful."

"You'll love Colleen." Green sparks of excitement lit up Hannah's eyes. "She's the head of the Brigade. She and her husband raise quarter horses on their ranch. As soon as we arrive home, I'll talk to her."

When the kitchen phone rang, Zane resented the interruption, but got up from the chair to answer it. He assumed it was one of the crew calling to thank Meg for the stollen she'd insisted on making for them.

While everyone continued talking in the background, he picked up the receiver and said Merry Christmas.

"Mr. Broderick?"

It was a female voice he didn't recognize. Probably one of Meg's friends or family from out of town. "Speaking."

"This is Mrs. Eisner from social services."

Zane had been told they would stop by for periodic checkups. But surely they wouldn't come on Christmas night.

"Yes? What can I do for you?"

"I wouldn't normally phone at this hour, especially on a holiday, but there's been a development you need to know about. In cases like yours, the law demands we move quickly."

Feeling like someone had just slammed a boulder into his gut, he turned his back to Meg. "What development?"

"A teenage girl who claims to be Baby Doe's birth-mother, turned up at the Tooele police department with her parents last week. She swears her boyfriend stole the baby from her, and she wants it back.''

Suffocating pain made it difficult for Zane to breathe.

''She has obtained a lawyer who ordered DNA testing done. He subpoenaed the police records for the tests done on the baby. Our office received a fax just before closing yesterday. It proves conclusively that she's the mother of the child.''

Dear God.

''Under the circumstances, her attorney is pushing for a hearing before the judge, day after tomorrow at ten a.m.''

He clutched the receiver in a deathlike grip. That was only thirty-six hours from now!

''You and your wife are required to be there with the baby. Knowing your plans to adopt, this office is fully aware of the pain you will suffer should the judge rule in the birthmother's favor.

''No matter how much you were warned that this possibility could occur, no one is ever fully prepared for the inevitable heartbreak. That's the reason for my phone call. To help you deal with the shock before you have to appear in court.

''Because this will be a highly emotional situation, I suggest you retain legal counsel to represent you before the judge. I must also advise you to take an extra change of clothing, diapers and formula in case the judge grants the mother immediate temporary custody.''

''*He could do that?*''

''If he feels moved to render such a decision, then yes. I've seen it happen before. On the other hand, if he isn't satisfied with the evidence presented, he will allow you to go on giving temporary foster care until such a time as she's ready to come before the court again to petition for permanent custody."

Zane prayed he would wake up from this nightmare. But to his horror, he could still hear her voice talking on the other end of the line.

"I'm sorry to be the bearer of such bad news on Christmas, Mr. Broderick. Out of consideration for you and your wife, I waited until the day was almost over."

When he thought back over their glorious holiday thus far, he realized she'd done them a favor. If there were any way to keep this news from Meg, he would do it. But that wasn't possible.

"Thank you, Mrs. Eisner." He hung up the receiver, dreading what he had to do.

The room had grown silent.

"Zane? Was that your parents?" Meg asked in a tremulous voice.

He felt a thousand years old as he turned around to face his adorable wife. The anxiety in her eyes almost defeated him.

How was he going to tell her?

"If the rest of you will excuse us for a minute, I need to talk to Meg in the living room."

CHAPTER EIGHT

"THAT phone call was about Johnny, wasn't it."

She'd followed him into the hallway, but no further. He braced himself against the wall and reached for her hands.

"Did the police find the birthmother?"

Heaven help me.

"Don't tell me she wants Johnny back?" Her question reverberated along the corridor.

"I'm afraid so," he finally answered in a tortured whisper.

"No." She started shaking her head. "No, Zane." She clutched his hands so tightly her nails dug into his skin, but he knew she wasn't aware of it. "Not now. She can't do that to us now!"

Her grief shattered him.

When she broke down in great heaving sobs, he crushed her in his arms, trying to relieve her pain. But the longer he held her, the more she refused to be comforted.

"He's our little boy. He loves us and would be frightened with anyone else. Johnny—" She cried his name.

Breaking free of Zane's hold, she ran down the hall toward the nursery. By the time he'd caught up to her, she'd gathered their sleeping baby in her arms.

Her beautiful face glistened with tears. "She didn't want him, Zane. He was left outside to die. What kind of a mother would let that happen? We're not going to give him up!''

Her wild-eyed gaze made him realize the news had sent her into shock. Convulsed as she was, he didn't dare tell her that the baby had apparently been stolen.

She carried their sleeping child to the living room, cradling him against her heart. Zane motioned to Blaire and Hannah who'd come out of the kitchen. They wanted to know what they could do to help.

"Would you girls sit with Meg for a minute while I call the hospital?"

"Of course."

Zane thanked them, then hurried over to the phone to call the ER. Dr. Parker was on duty. As soon as he heard what had happened to Meg, he said he would phone the hospital pharmacy for a sedative. It would knock her out and help her sleep.

That was exactly what she needed.

"I'll go pick it up," Alik offered after Zane hung up the phone.

"Thanks, bud."

Dominic clasped Zane's shoulder. "Tell me everything."

It was a relief to unburden himself. When he'd finished, Dom pulled out his cell phone. In a matter of minutes, the conversation came to an end and Dom turned to him.

"That was Len Wiseman, my private attorney and long-time friend from New York. I'm flying him out tomorrow in the company jet. He said he would phone you on his way to the airport in the morning so you can brief him on the particulars.

"In the meantime he wants us to sit down and work

out the most convincing defense you can construct for the judge. We'll do it after Meg falls asleep.''

Zane nodded. ''Thank God you're all here.'' He raked an unsteady hand through his hair. ''This is something I was told could happen, but I never really believed it. Neither of us did. Meg's in total denial.''

''My wife would have reacted the same way,'' Dom stated. ''Hannah not only fought for the right to keep Elizabeth forever, she braved a raging forest fire to rescue someone else's boy. I'll never be surprised again at the lengths some women are willing to go in the name of mother love.''

''It *was* instant love when Meg set eyes on Johnny.''

''For you, too, *mon ami*. If Len can't sway the judge in your favor, no one can. Tomorrow, Meg will be more herself. Len has an amazing way of reassuring his clients.''

''I don't know, Dom. If we end up losing Joh—''

''If that should happen,'' Dom interrupted him firmly, ''and mind you it's way too soon to even be talking about such an eventuality, then get her pregnant as soon as possible. We'll clear out of here tomorrow so you can have your privacy back. Let the honeymoon continue.''

Dom had a way of reading Zane's mind, but he didn't know all the facts. Zane stared at him for a minute. ''You mean, *begin*.''

His friend's intelligent eyes darkened in comprehension. ''*Mon Dieu*. After that kiss in the liv—''

''Our first,'' Zane muttered.

Dom shook his head incredulously. ''All the more reason Alik and I are going to gather our families and fly back in the company jet tomorrow.

"We'll meet Len at the airport and give him the keys to our rental car. He can drive to Tooele and come straight here. After we touch down in Denver, I'll instruct the pilot to fly the jet back to Salt Lake."

A sound at the back door interrupted them. It was Alik.

"Here you go." He handed Zane the pills. "I ran into Dr. Tingey on my way out of the pharmacy. When I told him about Meg, he gave me some advice for you.

"Apparently she hates medication of any kind, so you're going to have to force her to take it. He also said one pill won't be enough to start with. She'll need two tonight, and one every four hours beginning tomorrow morning. He wants her to take them for at least three days."

Zane nodded. "What would I do without you guys?"

"Let's hope none of us ever has to find out," Dom muttered.

Alik clapped Zane on the shoulder. "We'll turn in so you can be alone with Meg. Good luck tonight."

"Thanks."

As they left, he went to the fridge for a soda. Ginger ale was her favorite. On impulse, he put three pills in his other hand, then headed for the living room where everyone was saying goodnight.

Meg sat there white-faced, rocking the baby. Zane could tell she was making a valiant attempt to be cordial to their friends, but her heart was breaking.

He stood behind the others and waited until it was just the two of them and the baby. "I have some good news, Meg."

Hope sprang in her red-rimmed eyes. "What is it?"

"Dom has hired his own private attorney to help us. His name is Len Wiseman. He'll be flying in tomorrow and wants to meet with us as soon as he gets here."

"That's very kind of Dominic, but I was hoping you meant something else."

"This man is going to do everything in his power to convince the judge we should keep Johnny. When he arrives, he'll meet with us here at the house to plan a strategy. That's why I want you to take these tablets. Alik went over to the hospital for them."

"What are they?"

"A sedative Dr. Tingey says will help you to cope for the next couple of days."

"I don't want any pills. I just want Johnny." Tears gushed out of her eyes once more.

"So do I, Meg. But if we fall apart now and lose our sleep, we won't be in any shape to meet with Mr. Wiseman, let alone appear in court as two emotionally-stable parents."

"Did he prescribe them for you, too?"

Her question played right into his hands. "Yes," he lied. If he could take her to bed and love her the way he wanted, it would be a more potent healer than any drug. "I'll take mine first."

He popped one in his mouth and took a swig of ginger ale without swallowing the pill. She needed someone watching over her tonight.

"Your turn."

At first he thought she would push his hand away, but after a moment, she put them both in her mouth and drank from the can.

Relieved it hadn't come to her refusing him altogether, he got up and pulled out the Hide-A-Bed opposite the couch. He put the pill in his pocket at the same time.

"Come on." He half carried her across the expanse. "Just lie down here with Johnny. That's it." He removed her shoes, then pulled the covers over them before turning off the light. Only the glow of the Christmas tree remained.

"Don't leave us, Zane."

"I have no intention of going anywhere," he murmured. "In fact, I'm going lie right here next to our son. When he wakes up for his bottle, I'll get it."

"Thank you," she whispered in a tear-filled voice.

Her bouts of weeping almost destroyed him, but eventually they subsided, and after a while he could hear the kind of sounds that told him she was out for the rest of the night.

Thank God.

Afraid either of them could roll over on the baby if they fell asleep, he carried Johnny to the nursery and put him in his crib. He wasn't due another bottle for at least an hour.

With everyone in the house settled down, he tiptoed back to the living room and lay down on top of the covers by Meg. They were both turned toward each other. Only a few inches separated them. He studied each lovely feature until it was time for the baby's next feeding.

The medicine Meg had taken must have been powerful. When he came back to bed a half hour later, she was still in the same position as before, her silky hair splayed across one of his pillows.

His arms ached to draw her against him. On a final groan, he moved on his other side, willing sleep to come.

*　*　*

"All rise. The Second District Court of Tooele County, Utah, is now in session. Judge Malcolm Anderson presiding."

Zane helped Meg to her feet. He didn't think the baby had left her arms since she'd awakened yesterday morning. Constant, excruciating pain had replaced her hysteria of the previous night.

She'd refused to take any more medicine. But Zane had come to the conclusion that no pill could erase her suffering, or his...

Johnny had become their son. In their hearts, he *was* their son.

"You may be seated."

A group of people were assembled behind the opposition's table, including a short, slightly overweight teenage girl. She had a nice-looking face and light brown hair swept back in a ponytail. Zane presumed she was the birthmother.

"There she is," Meg whispered in agony.

"I can see her." He tightened his arm around her shoulders.

Since the phone call from Mrs. Eisner, Meg had constantly turned to him, the way a wife did a husband. Only one thing was missing to make their marriage real...

"Remember what Mr. Wiseman told us. Keep our focus on him and don't react to anything the other attorney might say."

"I—I won't."

At the airport, Dominic had warned the attorney that Meg didn't know the young girl had made a claim about her baby being stolen. When Mr. Wiseman arrived, the first thing he did was tell Meg that in these cases it was common for the birthmother to make up lies, either to protect the birthfather, herself, another family member, or all of the above.

Whatever story was presented in court, Meg needed to maintain a composed facade. If Mr. Wiseman did his job right, the judge would still rule that it was in the best interests of the child to remain in the care of the foster parents.

Relieved because the attorney's explanation had gone a long way to reassure both Meg and Zane, he was able to phone Dominic last night while Meg was feeding the baby and express his gratitude for all Dom's help.

The judge pounded his gavel. "In the Show Cause Hearing of Walton versus the State of Utah State Division of Child and Family Services, counsel for the Plaintiff, Mr. Farr, will now approach the bench."

"Your Honor, I'm here today representing my six-teen-year-old client, Cindy Walton, the daughter of Mr. and Mrs. Joseph Walton, who resides at 3270 Lakeland Drive in Salt Lake.

"Cindy met the birthfather of her baby at a rock concert at Saltair, and began seeing him without her parents' knowledge. When she told him she was pregnant, he told her to get rid of it or he wouldn't have anything more to do with her.

"It broke her heart because she was in love with him and wanted to have his baby. As soon as her parents found out she was expecting, they forbid her to see him again and got counseling for her. It was decided she would give up the baby for adoption.

"Near the end of her pregnancy, my client, still brokenhearted, took one of the family cars without permission and went to see her seventeen-year-old boyfriend, Shane Dibble, at his parents' ranch located at

Star Route Three outside Tooele. She hoped he would have changed his mind about the baby, and they could get married.

"It was evening. They drove behind the barn where no one would see them. But her labor had already started and she gave birth while they were together.

"Instead of getting her to a hospital, he put her back in the car, then took the baby. Before he ran off, he warned her that if she told anymore what had happened, he would come after her.

"In her traumatized condition, she eventually drove home, but was terrified to tell her family anything. She kept up the pretense of being pregnant for the next twenty-four hours, but when her mother discovered she was bleeding, she took her to the doctor.

"At that point in time my client told her parents the truth. They immediately called the police and there was a warrant issued for Mr. Dibble's arrest. But by then he'd already left town and his family was looking for him.

"When her parents realized how much she wanted to keep her baby, they told her that if it could be found, they would help her raise it until she was old enough to earn a living and take care of it herself.

"The news of Baby Doe showing up at the Oquirrh Mountains Medical Center led the Waltons to contact my Salt Lake office and I put in a call to the State Division of Child and Family Services. A DNA test was done on Baby Doe, matching it with the birth-mother.

"It's the wish of my client, Cindy Walton, and her parents who offer full financial, emotional, physical and spiritual backing, that Baby Doe be returned to his rightful mother who never stopped wanting this baby, and has suffered untold anguish over the way it was stolen from her at the very moment of birth.''

Zane didn't need to look at Meg to know the attorney's opening arguments had shaken her. He could only hope she remembered Mr. Wiseman's advice about not jumping to conclusions before they knew the real facts.

"This is only the beginning," he whispered near her ear. She nodded, but beneath his arm, he could tell her body had gone rigid with fear.

"Thank you, Mr. Farr. You may step down. The court wishes to call Mr. Wiseman, Counsel for the Defense, to the bench."

"Thank you, Your Honor. My clients, Mr. and Mrs. Zane Broderick, residing at 1017 Parkway in Tooele, are the legal, temporary foster parents for Baby Doe as decreed by the Utah State Division of Child and Family Services in a court of law.

"In their care the boy is thriving, as evidenced by the medical reports I shall enter as Exhibit A. Visits to their home by Mrs. Eisner who represents the state's right to custody of the child, reflect the perfect care given this infant, as evidenced by her report which I shall enter as Exhibit B.

"The birthmother's heart-wrenching story has struck a vulnerable chord in everyone in this courtroom. But I wish we knew the *whole* story, Your Honor.

"After undergoing counseling, the client agreed she would give up her baby for adoption. If her mind was definitely made up, why did she drive to Tooele to see Mr. Dibble when he'd told her they were finished?

"We all know the reason. It's the most natural one in the world. She was hoping the birthfather would have suffered a change of heart, that he would want her back and the three of them could be a family.

"Who could blame her for wanting that? A sweet, young, hopeful girl of sixteen, desiring a husband and baby of her own."

"But therein lies the problem. Without the birth-father in the picture, we don't know if she truly wants to take on the lifetime responsibility of loving and caring for this baby. That's a very difficult decision for anyone to make, let alone a minor.

"I understand Mr. Dibble, also a minor, the young man she loved up until recently, and probably still loves and forgives, is in the custody of the Nevada police department, waiting to be extradited to Utah for arraignment.

"Pending the outcome of his eventual trial for attempted murder, and negligence toward the victim which could have resulted in a manslaughter charge, I submit that Ms. Walton couldn't possibly know her own mind at this precarious and emotional moment in time. Under the circumstances, who could?

"In the best interests of the baby, I request that the court order a psychiatric evaluation on Ms. Walton and more counseling to ascertain her true motivation for wanting to keep her child."

"Objection, Your Honor! She's already been in counseling."

"Objection overruled, Mr. Farr. Your client went back on her decision to give up the baby for adoption." The judge pounded his gavel. "Proceed, Mr. Wiseman."

"I furthermore request that the entire Walton family attend counseling with their daughter to explore their deepest feelings before they take on the rearing of another family member. Raising a new baby in their household with other siblings will require a group effort that won't be easy.

"In the interim, I respectfully request that the Brodericks be allowed to continue nurturing the baby who has known nothing but the love and security of both foster parents from the moment he was brought into the emergency room by Mr. Broderick."

The judge nodded. "Thank you, Mr. Wiseman. You may step down.

"This hearing was brought before the court to show cause why the birthmother should be given custody of her baby.

"I've heard the arguments on both sides. The court is aware of the baby's need to bond with the birthmother as soon as possible, if she's going to be given custody.

"Nevertheless, I tend to agree that the plaintiff and her parents could benefit from more counseling before a final decision is made.

"Therefore, I hereby order that the plaintiff and her parents go in for immediate individual and family counseling to be carried out by a reputable counseling service provided through the state office under Mrs. Eisner's recommendation.

"In a month, all parties will reconvene in this courtroom to hear the opinion of the psychiatrist. At that time I'll render my verdict.

"During the interim, the baby will remain in the temporary custody of the foster parents.

"Both counselors are now free to confer upon a date and discuss the appropriate counseling service with Mrs. Eisner.

"Court is adjourned."

While Mr. Wiseman approached the other attorney, a euphoric Zane kissed the side of his wife's pale face. "We won, Mrs. Broderick."

"No we didn't, Zane." Her voice shook before the tears poured down her cheeks. "Everything's still temporary."

"Look at me," he demanded softly. She lifted pain-filled brown eyes to him. "Don't you understand? That girls' parents came to court prepared to take Johnny home with them. But Mr. Wiseman's genius threw them a curve. It bought us four more weeks with our son."

He could see her throat working. "You're right. I'm being horrible when I ought to be getting down on my knees to that man."

"Dominic said he was the best."

She wiped her eyes. "Forgive me. I *am* grateful we get to take our son home."

"He's going to *stay* our son," he murmured against her lips before she could bury her face in Johnny's neck.

But the death of Zane's brother had taught him never to take anything for granted. Starting tonight, he was going to work on getting his wife pregnant. Now that they'd won this round, it was all he could think about.

"Come on. Let's thank Mr. Wiseman and see him off to the airport. Then we'll phone your parents and invite them over to help us eat all the leftovers."

"They'd love that." She sounded a little happier than before.

"I'll make a fire and we can show them the video we took."

He was looking forward to that. But he was looking forward to something else even more.

Before his friends had left for the airport, Dominic had placed a video in his hand. The one Dom had taken. Alik stood by with a knowing smile.

"There's something on this you have to see, *mon ami*." Three gazes met in silent understanding. "Just remember, I want it back for posterity's sake."

As soon as they'd seen Meg's parents to the door, she'd gone into the bathroom, ostensibly to get ready for bed. But it was the growing shame over her own pathetic behavior the last few days that had driven her to hide from Zane now that they were alone.

He thought he'd married a strong, stable, capable woman. Instead, she'd turned into a walking nervous breakdown at the first sign of trouble.

Meg was humiliated to realize that since the ghastly phone call from Mrs. Eisner on Christmas night, she'd acted as if no one else existed but the baby.

Because she'd fallen apart, their friends had left Tooele earlier than planned. But the worst thing she'd done was to shut Zane out by taking over the baby. Never once had she considered his pain.

She'd behaved like a madwoman, the kind books were written about.

Appalled by her actions, she couldn't let another minute go by without apologizing. It wouldn't undo the damage. Nothing could do that. But her conscience wouldn't let her stay silent a moment longer.

Cinching the belt of her terry-cloth robe a little tighter around the waist, she left the bathroom and went in search of him. She thought he might be putting the baby down, so she went to the nursery first, to check.

Johnny lay sound asleep in his crib.

She'd taken so long in the bathroom, Zane had probably gone to bed, too. The emotional events of the last few days had no doubt taken their toll on him, wiping him out.

Still, he might not be asleep yet.

As she approached his door, which had been left ajar, she heard noise coming from the living room. Maybe she was wrong and he'd passed out watching the news on TV.

To her surprise he was sitting in the easy chair, glued to the television. But it wasn't a program he was watching so intently. It was a video. At first she thought it was the one she'd taken.

As she moved closer to get a better look she heard Dominic say, *"Eh bien, mon ami,* a kiss for posterity would be in order about now, *n'est-ce pas?"*

Suddenly the camera zoomed in on Meg and Zane.

What she saw turned her face scarlet because it meant that their friends had witnessed something never meant for another soul to see.

Had any woman ever returned a man's kiss with more passion?

Embarrassed and out of breath, she walked in front of him and turned off the set.

Swinging around she said, "Zane? Forgive me for interrupting, but there's something I have to say to you before I go to bed."

Though his eyes were shuttered, she could still feel the vibrancy of his blue gaze as it wandered over her.

He lounged back in the chair, drawing her attention to his hard-muscled physique and powerful legs which were extended. The dying embers from the fire, plus the lights on the tree, picked up the gold highlights in his dark-blond hair.

"Go right ahead."

This close to him, it was impossible to concentrate. Swallowing hard, she moved to the couch and sat down. To her consternation, he got up from the chair.

In the next breath he'd walked over and seated himself next to her, extending his arm along the back where it brushed against her hair. The contact sent trickles of longing through her body.

"What did you want to talk about?"

She bowed her head, attempting to fight her awareness of him. "I hardly know where to start."

"That sounds rather ominous."

"No— I mean—" She clasped her hands together nervously. "I didn't intend for you to think something was wrong."

Now that he'd come over to the couch, this wasn't going to work. She rose to her feet, reaching for an empty baby bottle sitting on the coffee table.

With it grasped in her hand like a lifeline, she turned to face him. "I—I owe you an apology," she stammered.

His body didn't move. "For what?"

"For behaving like a demented woman."

"What are you talking about?"

"You don't have to pretend. I know how awful I've been, and I'm so ashamed."

"Why?" He sounded perplexed. "What is it you think you've done?"

"Oh, I *know* what I've done. Ever since Mrs. Eisner phoned, I've been like a deranged lunatic. The way I've acted, the way I've shut you out and clung to the baby as if he were mine alone, my behavior has been unconscionable.''

The tears had started again, but she was powerless to stop them.

"Everything that's happened since we learned we had to be in court has been about *me*.

"I really went to pieces." Her voice wobbled. "Otherwise you wouldn't have felt it necessary to call the doctor and get something to calm me down.

"Our poor friends—here they came for a lovely Christmas holiday, and I just let them walk out of here two days before they were supposed to leave.

"But what's the most terrible of all, I kept the baby to myself, as if you didn't have any part in his life. *You*, who found him, and loved him, and wanted to adopt him, couldn't pry him away from me if your life had depended upon it.''

She shook her head, sobbing. "I'm so sorry, Zane. Can you ever forgive me?''

"There's nothing to forgive." The next thing she knew, she was in his arms. "You acted exactly like a mother who loves her child," he murmured into her hair. "If your feelings for Johnny hadn't been that strong from the beginning, you would never have consented to become my wife.''

"But you're Johnny's father. I wasn't thinking of your needs when I commandeered him."

He laughed deep in his throat. "That's nonsense.''

She buried her face against his shoulder. "No, it isn't. But I promise you, I'll never act that way again, whatever happens.''

His hands moved up and down her back, urging her closer. "We're not going to lose him.''

"I pray not," she responded emotionally. "But if

the judge does decide in the birthmother's favor, I swear I won't fall apart until I'm alone where no one will see me."

"We're not even going to think like that." He slid his hands to her upper arms and put her far enough away from him that he could look into her eyes. "What's important is that we start planning for a little brother or sister for Johnny right away."

What?

"I was raised from the cradle with a twin and loved it. You had siblings. We don't want Johnny to grow up an only child. He's going to need a little buddy, be it a boy or a girl. How would you feel about that?" His voice had grown husky.

She wasn't certain she'd heard him correctly. "You really want another baby for Johnny?" Her voice sort of squeaked.

"More than anything in the world."

There was a tone in his voice that told her he meant what he was saying with every fiber of his being.

They would have *two* babies to love. She had to be dreaming.

"How soon could we start adoption proceedings?" she cried out in excitement.

Through the material of her robe, the heat from his hands kneading her flesh sent a river of desire through her sensitized body.

A devastating half smile broke the corner of his mouth. "I wasn't thinking adoption."

Her thoughts reeled. "If you're talking about smuggling one of those orphan babies out of a foreign country, I couldn't do it. The law would eventually catch up with us. We'd not only lose our babies, we'd be put in prison!"

"That isn't what I had in mind, either," he said in his low, captivating voice. "There's another process you obviously haven't thought of. One that doesn't involve attorneys or agencies. No third parties of any kind. It only requires the two of us."

CHAPTER NINE

"Doctor? What did you find when you got in there?"

"Both ovaries were diseased."

"So I don't have any now?"

"I'm sorry, Meg. But you still have your life."

"What life? I'll never be able to have children."

"One day you might look after another woman's children, or you might adopt."

"I'm no longer a woman."

"You'll always be able to enjoy a full sexual relationship with the man you marry."

"A man instinctively chooses the woman who can give him babies."

"Tell that to the millions of men who've loved and married infertile women."

"Dear God, I wish I'd died on that operating table."

"One day you'll thank God you didn't. Now I'm going to give you something to help the pain so you can sleep."

Meg never had any intention of lying to Zane.

They'd both entered the marriage with the understanding that it was in name only.

Now it seemed he was willing to change the rules, and she knew why. In case they couldn't keep Johnny, he wanted a baby from their bodies so no one could ever take it away from them.

Her heart ached for Zane. For the loss of his brother.

153

For the possible loss of their little boy to his birth-mother in a month.

More than anything in her life, she wanted to give Zane his own child to love. *Their own child.* But it wasn't possible...

"Why aren't you saying anything?" he whispered against her lips. "You know what I'm asking. It's all I've been able to think about in weeks. I've almost gone out of my mind living this close to you, aching for you. Let me love you, Meg."

Before she could stop him, his mouth closed over hers with smothering force. The second she felt the driving force of his need, she never wanted him to stop.

Since their kiss the other night, her body had yearned to know his full possession. With no guests in the house and the baby asleep, she could finally give in to the clamoring demands of her body.

The way he touched and caressed her, the taste of his mouth, it filled her with such rapture she moaned in ecstasy. There was no way to tell where one kiss ended and the next one began. She couldn't think while their bodies molded to each other, hungrily striving to become one flesh.

Scarcely cognizant of being carried to his bedroom, all she knew was that he had set her on fire and now she couldn't get enough of him.

"Help me," he cried as his hands went to the tie of her robe. "I want you so badly, I'm trembling."

Her robe slid to the floor, then she was on the bed, their arms and legs entwined while they devoured each other.

At one point he relinquished her mouth long enough

to capture her flushed face between his hands. His eyes burned a hot blue as he looked down at her.

"You're incredibly beautiful, Meg. You could have no idea how I've longed to make a baby with you. Now that we have Johnny, how about we try for a little girl with deep velvety brown eyes that can melt a man's heart, just like yours melted mine in the ER."

Groaning inwardly, she grasped his wrists before he could remove his hands from her face. "In your own masculine way, you're every bit as gorgeous, Zane. In all honesty, you're the most attractive man I've ever met in my life.

"I would be lying if I told you I didn't desire you with every cell in my body. Having said that, there's something you need to know before this goes any further."

He didn't move, but lines suddenly darkened his handsome face, making him look older than his thirty-four years.

"There's someone else you can't get out of your heart." His voice grated.

"No. I never lied to you. But I withheld some information that I didn't expect would ever be relevant. Now it is," she whispered in agony.

With that answer, he removed his hands and sat up on one elbow. Meg took advantage of the moment to slide off the bed. Though her nightgown still covered her, she reached for her bathrobe and put it on.

His eyes narrowed on her face. "Nothing you say is going to change the fact that I want you back in my bed as soon as you get this off your chest."

"That's where you're wrong, Zane," came her dampening response.

Something in her tone must have told him this was

serious. He grimaced before levering himself from the bed.

"What is it?"

She struggled not to break down. "All my life I wanted to be a mother more than anything else in the world. The gods must have heard me. A few years ago I had to have an operation with the result that you and I could make love until kingdom come, but you would never be able to impregnate me."

His eyes grew bleak, but she kept on talking because once she stopped, the tears would fall like the downpour of a tempest.

"When you asked me to marry you in name only, I saw it as my chance to be a mother to Johnny. Knowing you had no expectations of me, I didn't feel there was any reason to tell you I was sterile.

"But because I went hysterical on you after Mrs. Eisner called, you came up with the idea to get me pregnant in case we lose Johnny. Believe me, if I could give us a child, I would." Her voice throbbed.

"However now that you know the circumstances, we'll both be glad we didn't consummate our marriage.

"Should the judge rule in Cindy Walton's favor, then there'll be no more reason for us to stay married. With a quick divorce, you'll be free to find a woman who can give you a child. If ever anyone was meant to be a father, you are, Zane.

"Right now I could line you up with at least ten women I know who are beautiful, intelligent, single and able to bear children. That's why it would be better if we avoid any more physical involvement.

"To be honest, I'd rather we walked away from each other as good friends who shared in the love of one precious little boy who needed us to care for him until his mother could.''

His features looked chiseled. ''You talk as if the judge has already made up his mind to give Johnny back to the birthmother.''

''Naturally I'm hoping that doesn't happen. But since both of us have undergone painful life-changing experiences in the past, we've learned not to take anything for granted.

''Still, until the next hearing I'm going to take your advice and not think negative thoughts. If or when they take Johnny away from us, then will be the time that I find out what I'm really made of.

''Goodnight, Zane.''

For the rest of the night Meg waited for him to come to her room and tell her that he loved her, that whatever happened in the future, they would work things out because he couldn't bear to lose her.

It wasn't until the baby's morning feeding that she cried her heart out because he hadn't made an appearance. Her pain became acute when she discovered he'd left for work without saying goodbye.

It set a precedent for the next three weeks. They behaved like polite strangers, or more appropriately, employer and nanny. She fixed his meals, cleaned his clothes and his house. They took turns loving and caring for Johnny, but beyond that, there was little communication.

Their friends in Laramie called every other day to lend their support. Meg's parents came by often and phoned on a regular basis. Meg's friends at the hospital stayed in touch, adding their encouragement.

When a phone call came midmorning three weeks

later, Meg wasn't prepared to hear Mrs. Eisner's voice on the other end.

"Mrs. Broderick? I'll get right to the point. The judge has ordered that the baby be allowed an overnight visit with the Waltons. They're going to come for him at three o'clock today, and will have him back by three tomorrow."

A pain pierced Meg's heart, almost incapacitating her.

"Therefore you need to bring the baby to our office by two o'clock with all the things he'll need for an eighteen-hour period, including formula of course. They'll have a car seat and a crib.

"Tomorrow I'll phone you when they've brought the baby back so you can come and get him straight away. Do you know where we're located?"

"Yes."

"Very good. Then I'll see you at two."

Numb with pain, Meg hung up the receiver.

The horror story was beginning.

"Hey, Zane? You're wanted on the phone."

"Who is it?"

"Your wife."

If that was Meg, then there was some kind of emergency because she sure as hell wouldn't be calling him for any other reason.

When she'd admitted she couldn't have children, all the pieces of the puzzle fell into place. It wasn't love for him, but the driving need to be a mother to Johnny, that had prompted her to accept his marriage proposal.

Telling her about his brother had only succeeded in bringing out her compassionate instincts. If he'd pushed for it, he had no doubts he could have made love to her anytime in the last three weeks. Apparently her sacrifice knew no bounds.

But the thought of her sharing his bed for any other reason than love pained him in ways he couldn't bring himself to examine yet. Not when there was still a week to go before Johnny's future was decided.

An unaccountable feeling of dread took over as he left the control room and hurried into his office to get the phone.

"Meg? Is there something wrong with Johnny?" he asked without preamble.

"No, but Mrs. Eisner phoned. The baby has to go on an overnight visit to the Waltons. We have to take him to the social services office by two o'clock today. C-could you come, please?"

He closed his eyes tightly. Whenever he heard that tremor in her voice, it got him right in the gut. "I'll be there in five minutes."

"Martin?" he called to his assistant.

"Yeah, boss?"

"I've got to go home. You're in charge!"

The northern part of the state was enjoying its yearly January thaw. The temperature was even warmer than when Zane had come to work. By afternoon it would probably climb into the fifties.

He got in the truck and started the motor. If he closed his eyes so he couldn't see the snow-swept mountain peaks, he could almost believe it was spring. Today was the kind of day to get out and enjoy with his family. What a cruel irony!

Everything looked blurry as he drove hell-bent for home. He could just imagine the state Meg would be in by the time he entered the house. But he had to reassess his thinking when he found her and the baby in the living room all dressed up, ready to go out.

She'd put Johnny in the colorful snowsuit and hat Alik and Blaire had given him for Christmas. The baby, more alert than ever before, had never looked more adorable. Zane couldn't resist giving him a long hug.

"It's so nice today, I thought we could drive to the center of town and take him for a walk in his stroller. I need to get a few more things to send with him.

"I thought we might stop somewhere for lunch, then drive him over to social services. I've got everything packed if you want to put the bags in the truck."

Not a sign of a tear anywhere, she'd dressed in the new navy cashmere sweater and tan wool pants he'd given her on Christmas morning. The breathtaking curves of her feminine figure made it difficult for him to keep his eyes off of her.

If a man could burst with pride over his family, Zane was a prime candidate as ten minutes later he pushed the stroller down the street with his gorgeous wife by his side.

No passerby seeing her beautiful face and lovely smile could guess that her heart was breaking into smaller pieces as each minute ticked away. But Zane knew because his heart was suffering the same agonizing turmoil.

Tonight would be the first night since they'd brought Johnny home that he wouldn't be with them, safely tucked in his crib.

By tacit agreement they didn't discuss what was going to happen in the next hour. Instead they enjoyed a pasta lunch served alfresco. Johnny lay propped in his stroller between them, sucking his pacifier with contentment.

On their way to the social services' office, Zane kept waiting for his wife to break down. But she seemed to have more control over her emotions than he did. In fact, when they had to hand Johnny over to Mrs. Eisner, Zane found himself relying on Meg's strength.

The second the baby left her arms, he began to cry. It wasn't his hungry wail. It was another kind that wrenched your gut open.

"Johnny's never been separated from us before," Meg explained in a surprisingly steady voice. "I think we'd better go, Zane. If he can't see or hear us, he'll quiet down a lot faster."

Mrs. Eisner nodded. "Being an ER nurse, you've probably been through this experience many times before."

The remark made him livid.

No, Mrs. Eisner. This is Johnny's mother you're talking to. She's never been through this experience before. Neither have I. It's killing both of us.

"I'll phone you tomorrow when it's time to pick him up," the older woman called to them. "You can plan on it being sometime between three and four o'clock."

No words passed between them on their way to the truck. Though Meg was still composed, her face had gone an unnatural white color.

"Zane?" she said his name the second they were inside the cab. "I hope you don't mind, but as soon as we get home, I'm planning to drive over to my folks' and spend the night."

It shouldn't have surprised him.

"I think it's a good idea." He lied through his teeth before putting the truck in gear.

At this point he wanted her to make a scene so he could comfort her. To his shock, she remained impassive. He didn't know how to deal with this kind of unspeakable grief.

"There's plenty of food in the fridge for dinner tonight. All you have to do is warm it up."

"I'll be fine."

"Expect me to be home around two-thirty tomorrow," she said as they turned in the driveway.

Her flight from the truck to the Jeep was swift and sure.

Thank heaven for clear weather. The second he lost sight of her taillights, he entered the house and phoned the small airport to charter a plane to Laramie. There was no way he was staying in this tomb alone tonight, surrounded by memories that were already tearing him apart.

No one was home when Meg let herself in her parents' house. Since they had no idea she was coming, her mother could be anywhere.

Needing something to do before she exploded with pain, she sat down at the upright piano and played an old tune. Halfway through it, she lost interest and gravitated to the study where she could watch TV.

Nothing appealed.

She turned it off and headed for her old bedroom, hoping she could fall asleep for a while. Five minutes later she knew it was hopeless and went to the kitchen for a soda to settle her churning stomach. Finding none, she made ice water, then poured it down the sink in revulsion.

Twenty minutes later she was still wandering aimlessly about.

Always before, she'd found comfort coming home. It had been her retreat, her place of refuge. Before today, a visit home would have made the world look a little brighter no matter how dark things appeared.

That's what home was supposed to do. That's what home *meant*.

But as she stood in the dining room where so much life had been lived, it hit her like a lightning bolt that this wasn't her home anymore.

She had her own home with Zane at 1017 Parkway.

Baby or no baby, it was the only home she wanted. Zane was the only man she wanted.

There were some fights you couldn't win. She would never be able to give birth. But she *could* fight for Zane's love. What a fool she'd been not to sleep with him when she'd had the chance.

The first thing she needed to do was drive home and tell him she loved him. She couldn't wait to tell him.

If they lost Johnny, then they would fight through their grief together and start the adoption process for another child. If Zane wanted a child from his own body badly enough, Meg would be more than willing for them to find a surrogate mother. Anything was possible if you loved enough.

By the time she'd reached Tooele, she was trembling with a mixture of fear and excitement. But her spirits plummeted when she realized his truck wasn't in the driveway.

He'd gone back to work of course. Where else would he go this time of day?

Unable to contain her emotions, she headed for his

work. To her bitter disappointment, his truck wasn't there, either.

He could be running an important errand. She had no choice but to go home and wait for him. As long as she had time on her hands, she would make him a dinner to die for.

When it got to be one in the morning and he still hadn't come home to eat or go to bed, she imagined he was staying overnight with a member of his crew.

She could drive around the town and find out, but it would serve no purpose since she wouldn't dare wake one of his co-workers and end up embarrassing Zane.

For the rest of the night, she lay on the couch and played the Christmas videos over and over again, feasting her eyes on the man and baby she adored.

The wind had picked up since Alik had driven Zane to the airport outside Laramie.

"The pilot is signaling that we need to take off. Thanks for letting me crash at your trailer last night without warning. Tell Blaire thanks again for making me feel so welcome."

"I will, but lest you forget, I've owed you big-time for how you helped bring Blaire and me together last fall."

"That was easy. Keeping you up all night while I told you my problems wasn't exactly a fair trade."

"Fair doesn't come into it. With the little guy's future still hanging in the balance, your life's already in hell without having the added pain of the situation with Meg. But you're going to do something about that when you get home. Right?"

Zane eyed his friend soberly before nodding. "I can't live like this any longer."

"If Dominic were here, he would tell you to do whatever it takes."

"I know."

Alik clasped his shoulder. "Keep me informed."

"Will do."

"Have a safe flight."

There'd been no word from Zane and it was going on three o'clock in the afternoon. Mrs. Eisner had already phoned to say the baby could be picked up at four.

Meg had started calling Zane's work early that morning, but no one had seen him. It finally dawned on her that he might have flown to Laramie.

She didn't start to panic until she couldn't reach the girls at the apartment or the trailer. All she could do was leave messages and pray either Dominic or Alik would call her back with some news.

At twenty to four she was ready to walk out the door when the phone rang.

She grabbed it after the first ring. "Hello?"

"Meg—"

It was Zane. "Thank God it's you! I've been worried sick."

"I'm sorry for leaving town without telling you."

Their connection was poor. "Where are you?"

"In Evanston, Wyoming."

So he *had* gone to Laramie...

"There's a new storm blowing in. The pilot decided to land here as a precaution. I've arranged for a rental car and will be home in about two hours."

Her body shook so hard in relief, she almost

dropped the receiver. "By the time you get here, Johnny will be back *home*."

"I'm sorry you have to go for him without me. I'll hurry."

She struggled for breath. "Please drive carefully."

"Don't worry. Give Johnny a hug and kiss for me."

"I will."

Euphoric because he would be home soon, she flew out the door, unable to get to social services fast enough. Luckily the building wasn't very far away. She got down from the Jeep and hurried inside the door.

Meg would know Johnny's cry anywhere. When she heard him clear at the other end of the hall, she started running.

"Mommy's here, sweetheart," she called out from the doorway. "I'm here, Johnny."

Mrs. Eisner looked relieved when Meg rushed across the room and plucked the baby right out of her arms.

"Oh, Johnny," she half sobbed his name before hugging him tightly against her chest. "I love you so much, my dear baby boy. I've missed you more than you'll ever know."

The baby stopped crying at once and nestled his face beneath her chin. Blessed quiet reigned in the office.

"Well—" Mrs. Eisner chuckled. "He certainly knows who his mother is. I'm glad you were on time. Otherwise everyone in the building would have been down here to find out what was going on."

Meg wanted to ask a thousand questions, but she knew Mrs. Eisner couldn't answer them.

"Come on, my little love. We're going home. You

can help me warm up the dinner I made for your daddy last night."

"I'll walk you out to your car with his things."

"Thank you, Mrs. Eisner."

Within ten minutes they'd arrived home in the Jeep. She spent the next half hour feeding him his bottle and loving him. Then she put him in his playpen which she'd set up by the kitchen table so he could watch her work.

At some point she heard a noise on the back porch. The sound of the door opening was like music to her ears. She spun around in time to see Zane walk in the kitchen.

He looked so wonderful she had to suppress the urge to fly across the room and throw her arms around his neck.

"I—I'm glad you're home." Her voice caught.

His gaze was all-consuming. "So am I," came the husky rejoinder.

"Johnny's been waiting and waiting for you."

"Is that so, little tiger. Well your daddy's here now." In a lithe movement, he leaned over and swept the baby from the playpen. "Let's sit down and have a talk, shall we? Your mommy and I want to hear all about your sleepover last night."

Meg turned toward the stove so he wouldn't see the tears his tender words had evoked.

"Hmm. It looks like we're going to be served another one of your mother's fabulous feasts. Bring it on. I'm famished!"

Needing no urging, Meg put everything on the table. With the baby still nestled against his broad shoulder, they tucked in.

"How are things in Laramie?"

"Excellent. Dom was in New York on business, so Blaire and Alik invited Hannah over to the trailer for dinner. Between little Nicky and Elizabeth, I was entertained all evening."

His eyes captured hers. "Did you have a nice time with your folks?"

It was truth time.

"I went over there for a while, then I came back."

He blinked. "You spent the night here?"

"Yes."

To her surprise he looked upset. "If I had known that, I would never have left town."

"I didn't know myself. Not until I got over there and realized I'd rather be *home*."

He rubbed the baby's back. "What did you do all evening?"

"I fixed this dinner, and then I watched videos."

"Meg—" he whispered. "I'm sorry. I had no idea."

"Please don't apologize. I was in such terrible shape after we dropped Johnny off, I didn't know what I wanted. Once more I was the selfish one who didn't stop to consider your pain. Naturally you would turn to your friends. They're practically family."

"They are. I'm a lucky man."

"Zane— C-can we talk frankly for a moment?"

"I thought that was what we were doing."

She drank some soda. "We are. I just meant that there's something important I have to say—no—I want to say to you. But I'm very nervous," she blurted.

"I can see that. Am I such an awful ogre, you're afraid of me?"

"No! Of course not." She bit her lip. "I know

you're dying to be with the baby. Why don't you get him ready for bed while I do the dishes. Then maybe we can really talk without any interruptions.''

"You must be reading my mind because there are some things I want to discuss with you, too.''

The unexpected comment unnerved her even more. She would make him talk to her first. Depending on the things he said, he could change what she'd planned to tell him.

"Come on, little tiger. Father and son missed their time together last night. How would you like to hear a story about Pooh Bear and the honey tree?''

Zane had a way with the baby that always moved her to tears. She needed to get over it, but she didn't know how.

Twenty minutes later she'd made the kitchen tidy and had started a wash. She couldn't tell what things in the baby's bags were clean, so she'd decided to do the whole load.

On her way in from the back porch, she heard the phone ring. Zane was putting the baby down so she hurried to answer it.

"Hello?''

"Mrs. Broderick?''

The male voice sounded somewhat familiar. "Yes?''

"This is Len Wiseman.''

A moan escaped her throat. He wouldn't be calling unless there was something wrong.

Her fingers twisted the phone cord without realizing it. "Yes, Mr. Wiseman. How are you?''

"I'm fine. Forgive me for calling you at this time of evening, but there's been a new development in your case. It's something you should know about immediately. Is your husband there?''

Meg could scarcely breathe. "Yes. Just a minute and I'll put him on the other line.''

"I'll wait.''

She left the receiver on the counter, then hurried out of the kitchen and down the hall to the nursery. When Zane saw her in the doorway beckoning to him, he tiptoed out of the room.

"Quick, Zane. It's Mr. Wiseman on the line. Pick up the extension in your room.''

"Is it bad news?''

"I don't know. I was too terrified to ask.''

Racing back to the kitchen, she put the receiver to her ear. "We're both on now, Mr. Wiseman.''

"Good. All right. Earlier this evening I had a call from the Waltons' attorney in Salt Lake. It seems that the counseling ordered by the court made an impact on the family, particularly on Cindy.

"After spending twelve hours with the baby, she admitted to her parents that she didn't really want to be a mother. All along it was the boyfriend she was after.

"The parents have no desire to raise the child when their daughter wants no part of it. So they're dropping the case. Tomorrow the family will meet with their attorney and they will sign a form that gives away all parental and grandparental rights.

"It won't be necessary for me to be with you in court. I'll send the papers by overnight courier to Mrs. Eisner at social services. She'll present them to the judge.

"Congratulations, you two. You are now the proud parents of a very lucky little boy. When the judge pounds his gavel, that baby will be yours for as long as you both shall live."

CHAPTER TEN

HIS words brought too much happiness to Meg's heart. While she tried to stifle her sobs, she had to rely on Zane who was still coherent enough to thank the attorney.

"We'll always be indebted to you, Mr. Wiseman. I'll courier you a check first thing in the morning."

"There's no need for that. Over the years, Dominic has played a big part in sending business my way. It's nice to be able to return the favor once in a while, especially in a cause as worthy as yours."

"My wife and I still insist. Someone else without your expertise wouldn't have been able to see the weakness in the girl's case. You've given us our lives." Zane's voice throbbed.

"You have!" Meg concurred. "Thank you from the bottom of our hearts, Mr. Wiseman."

"You're most welcome. Goodbye."

The second she heard the click, she made a dash for the hallway. Zane met her coming out of his bedroom. On his handsome face she saw the eager, tremulous smile of joy. It had turned him into a younger-looking man. She loved him so much...

"Zane—" Her voice caught.

"He's ours!"

Like a strong gravitational pull, they made their way into each other's arms. He lifted her off the ground and swung her around. She'd never heard such happy, unbridled laughter come out of anyone before.

His whipcord arms kept her in the air. "While I've got you where I want you, Mrs. Broderick, I want to hear the words."

The blue fire in his eyes sent her heart knocking against her chest. If she was wrong about this...

"Which ones, darling?"

"That's a start. Just don't stop."

"You mean, I love you?" Her voice trembled. With a satisfied groan, he lowered her to the floor. "Don't you know I fell in love with you the night you brought Johnny to the hospital?

"Like pure revelation, I knew you were the only man for me," she murmured on a ragged breath because he had started kissing the life out of her. "It's embarrassing to admit, but I would have done anything to be your wife."

"Keep going," he demanded, carrying her to his bed.

After he'd followed her down on the mattress, she cupped his face in her hands. "When I woke up from my operation, I told the doctor I wanted to die. He said that one day I would thank God I didn't.

"I'm thanking Him now, Zane." She covered his face with kisses, then found his mouth once more. "You know the adage about a door shutting, and a window opening?"

He nodded, staring deep into her soul.

"Someone got the phrasing wrong. It's an entire new universe that opens. It opened the universe to me when you swept into my life. I'm so in love with you, it terrifies me."

His expression grew solemn. "Within minutes of my arriving at the ER with Johnny, the two of you became *my* whole world. But it wasn't until the night

I was waiting for you to call me with your answer, and the phone never rang, that I knew real terror.

"It was the defining moment for me. Johnny or no Johnny, I had fallen in love with you and wanted you for my wife. But I was greedy and wanted him, too."

"Oh, Zane— I can't believe you love me." She wrapped her arms around his neck and clung to him.

"How could you have doubted it when I never left you alone? There was just one problem. We'd only known each other a week. If I'd told you I was in love with you, I was afraid it would have frightened you off. I couldn't afford to take that risk. So I used Johnny. Shamelessly, I might add."

"So did I," she whispered into his hair. "My parents were so upset when I told them I had married you. But as soon as I explained that I was desperately in love, they could see that all the reasoning in the world wasn't going to change my mind.

"It didn't take them long to understand why I had fallen so hard. They're crazy about you. Everyone is. I was euphoric when Johnny was well enough to leave the hospital and I could get you away from all those nurses, especially Julie."

His deep chuckle excited her. "Do you want to hear what I was about to do when I saw Jonah Ryder on our couch with his hands all over you?"

She kissed the side of his jaw. "I told you before. We didn't have that kind of relationship."

"From where I was standing, you could have fooled me. That night I learned the meaning of jealousy. It made me realize that I'd never truly been in love before."

"I don't understand that. You were engaged twice."

"Darling—the purpose of an engagement is to find

out if you want to be married. In both cases, I discovered that the most essential ingredient was missing. Then I met you.'' He kissed her long and hard. "What I felt for you was so powerful, I would have done anything to have you.''

"As Daddy said, I *did* do anything to belong to you.''

"Would you honestly have it any other way?'' came the fierce demand.

"No, Zane. Love needs to be that strong if two people are going to live together for a lifetime. Even so, I can't give you your own baby. Another woman cou—''

"Don't—'' He hushed her with his mouth. "I may not have fathered Johnny, but I can't imagine my feelings being any different for a child of my own body than the ones I have for him.

"To be truthful, when Dominic was telling Alik and me how anxious he is about Hannah's pregnancy, I felt guilty over my relief that I didn't have to worry about you going through that ordeal.

"It was bad enough waiting to see if Johnny would be all right. But it would have been a living hell if I'd had to fear for your life, too. I couldn't be happier to know that when we want to enlarge our family, we can adopt a baby that has already made its way into the world without putting your life in danger.''

From the fervency of his tone, the taut way he held his body while he was speaking, she could tell Zane meant what he said. He felt no deprivation.

"How was I lucky enough to find you?'' she cried emotionally.

"I've been asking the same question about you since the night this beautiful, fearless woman came to my defense in front of friend and foe. In that moment I knew I had to have you, or life would never hold the same meaning for me again."

She buried her face in his neck. "I gave myself away that night."

"Let's just say it strengthened my resolve to get you to marry me no matter how extreme the measures."

"If you noticed, I dropped everything to fly to Reno with you."

"You think I'll ever forget that day?" he asked in a husky voice.

"No." She pressed a hungry kiss to his mouth. "But we did it in such haste, we cheated a lot of people we love out of a wedding. I've been thinking about your parents."

He let out a deep sigh. "What about them?"

"Before you and I asked everyone to come for Christmas, Blaire confided that she and Hannah were worried how they were going to help their husbands get through the holidays without a lot of pain. She mentioned Alik's and Dominic's estrangement from their parents."

"She told you that?"

"Yes. Women tend to want the men they love to be happy. I—I don't think you're totally happy, Zane. How could you be when your family doesn't even know about Johnny or me."

She kissed the hand molding her cheek. "It hurt me for your sake that your parents didn't phone you over Christmas. But then I started wondering if they weren't waiting for you to reach out to them.

"Is it possible they regret having kept you at a distance all these years, and now it's just their pride standing in the way?"

Zane was quiet so long, she was afraid she'd made a fatal mistake in talking to him about this. But now that she'd broached the subject, she had to finish it.

"No matter what, they raised you to be the magnificent man you are. You can't tell me they wouldn't want to know that you're married and have a son.

"Darling? What if we asked them to attend Johnny's christening?"

His hands tightened in her silken hair. "They would never come."

"Maybe not, but will you give me permission to extend the invitation?"

"Next week when the judge makes Johnny legally ours, then I might be willing to discuss it."

Her heart raced. He hadn't said no.

"In the meantime, no more talk," he murmured, starting to remove her robe. "You could have no comprehension of the agony I've been through watching you disappear into your bedroom every night, knowing only a wall separated us.

"I'm warning you now, nothing will ever separate us again. I adore you, Meg. Don't you know I've been waiting a lifetime for you? Come here to me. Let me love you," he whispered urgently.

When Johnny didn't cry for his bottle until five in the morning, Meg wondered if their little boy knew this night had been different from all the others.

Although the doctor had told her she would function normally as a woman, she'd always retained a residual fear that she might disappoint her husband one day.

But hours of passion with Zane had removed any

worry in that department. Together they'd experienced indescribable rapture in the giving and taking of pleasure that made her feel immortal.

Languorous after their lovemaking, which hadn't ended until the early hours of the morning, she rebelled at the prospect of having to leave his solid warmth for any reason.

Only their baby had the power to separate her from the gorgeous male who'd finally fallen asleep. *He was gorgeous.* She still couldn't believe he was her husband, the man she had the right to love whenever she wanted.

Carefully she removed the strong arm that still held her hip in a possessive grip. It wasn't as easy to slide her leg out from under his, but somehow she managed.

Their bedroom was a disaster. While she stumbled around in the dark looking for her robe, the baby's cries grew more incessant.

In the normal scheme of things, a baby wasn't born until at least nine months after the honeymoon. It was a good thing Johnny was too young to see the result of what his daddy had done to her all night long.

She was a mess. A disheveled mess whose skin was tender from the rasp of Zane's beard. Just remembering what had gone on in his bed set her pulses throbbing.

After warming the baby bottle in the microwave, she hurried down the hall to the nursery.

"Here I am, little sweetie. Mommy's here."

Once his diaper was changed, she wrapped him in his quilt and started out the door to feed him in the living room.

"Where do you think you're going?"

She let out a tiny gasp as Zane slid his hands to her shoulders, pulling her against him.

"Darling—I was hoping you would stay asleep."

"Were you just?" he murmured, kissing her neck and shoulder in that way he had of enflaming her. "Come back to bed, my love. I don't like it in there without you."

His words produced another ache of desire she could do nothing about while their little boy needed her attention.

Once the baby was nestled between them devouring his formula, Zane leaned over to kiss her deeply on the mouth. "I finally have everything I want in life, right here where I want it."

"I'm so happy, it doesn't seem fair to anyone who isn't," she cried with yearning.

"I don't like that word. Let's just be thankful our son brought us together. Did you know he's more intelligent than most babies?"

Meg smiled. "Of course, but how did *you* find out?"

"Because he's aware his father can't wait to get his mother alone, and has finished his bottle in twice the normal amount of time. Come on, little tiger. Back to your crib."

A few minutes later her husband returned. As she felt his side of the mattress give, she reached for him with an eagerness that would make her blush when she thought about it later.

At ten, the phone disturbed them. She had no idea how long it had been ringing before Zane reached across her to pick up the receiver. Sated from making love during the early morning hours, they'd finally slept.

She could tell right away it was either Dom or Alik. The ring of pure joy in her husband's voice when he explained that they'd won custody of Johnny was something she would treasure in her heart forever.

He didn't stay on the phone long. The second he hung up, she felt his arms go around her.

"That was Dominic. He couldn't be happier for us and will spread the word."

"I think that's the shortest conversation you two ever had."

"He knew I was otherwise occupied."

Heat rushed into her cheeks. "How could he know something like that?"

"Our French friend has uncanny instincts."

"Darling? What did he ask before you said 'No. None'?"

A sudden stillness came over her husband.

Puzzled, she raised up on her elbow to look at him. To her shock, a film of moisture had darkened the blue of his eyes. Afraid she'd upset him in some way she cried, "Forgive me, Zane."

In the next instant he'd pulled her on top of him. "What are you talking about?"

"I didn't mean to pry. I know how close you are to your friends."

He sucked in his breath. "Let's get something straight right now. You're my wife. We share everything. You're entitled to know everything. Do you understand what I'm saying?"

She nodded. "Yes. I feel the same way."

He brushed her lips with his own. "Before we hung up, Dom asked if I'd had my usual nightmares last night."

When the significance of Zane's words sank in, tears filled Meg's eyes. "You mean—"

"I mean that when I did sleep, nothing disturbed it."

Overjoyed, she kissed the tears from his eyes. "Do you know what I think? I think your brother loves you so much, he had everything to do with sending little Johnny to us."

"After all that's happened, I'm beginning to think you could be right."

"I know I am. He wanted your suffering to end."

"What suffering?" He crushed her in his arms. "I don't know the meaning of that word anymore. I love you, Meg. Hold me. Never let me go."

She clung to her husband, touched to the depths of her soul by the vulnerability of this strong, marvelous man a blizzard had swept into her life, carrying their destiny in his arms.

EPILOGUE

"WHAT do you think of her, Hannah?"

The soft morning air was exhilarating as Meg rode her new quarter horse, Dancer, around the corral.

"She's a beauty! What a nice gait. Let's see her canter."

After putting Dancer—named for her four white stocking feet—through some fancy maneuvers for the next little while, Meg eventually headed for the bar of the fence where Hannah was leaning.

As she rode up to her, she could see her fully pregnant friend reaching around to rub her lower back again. She'd been doing that quite a lot while they'd been out here.

Day after tomorrow, May third, was Hannah's due date, but if her labor went fast, maybe this was going to be a May Day baby.

"How long has your back been hurting you like this?"

Hannah's green eyes flicked to hers in surprise. "I should have known I couldn't hide anything from you. It's been doing it on and off all night, but just now I felt some really powerful pains that came from the back to the front. They're beginning to sting like crazy!"

"Did you tell Dominic?"

"No! Please don't say anything to him! He's tried so hard to pretend everything's fine, but he's an absolute nervous wreck. I was so glad when you came by to get me out of the apartment.

"Lately every time he looks at me he loses color, goes unnaturally quiet, then dogs every footstep I take. Tending Elizabeth gives him something to do. Honestly, Meg, he's beginning to drive me— Oh! Here comes another one. *Oh boy!*"

Her friend clung to the bar while they both watched her stomach harden beneath her maternity blouse.

"That was a strong contraction, Hannah. I'd say you've been in labor a good ten hours already. I'm starting to time them. While I do that, I'll put Dancer away. Call out to me when it's over and the next one begins."

"Okay."

Meg slid off her horse and led her inside the barn. After removing the bridal, she gave her water and oats. Hannah shouted to her that another pain was starting. It looked like they were coming closer than five minutes apart. She might be close to being fully dilated.

By the time Meg went back and shut the door, Hannah cried, "My water just broke!"

"It sure did." Meg grinned at the puddle she'd made. "Be glad it happened out here with me."

"Oh, my gosh. If I'd done this in front of Dominic, he would have passed out with fright."

"And you wouldn't be able to rescue him on Cinnamon."

"No." Hannah smiled in remembrance of how she and Dominic first met, but then another pain started.

"Come on. I'll help you to the car. We're going to the hospital."

"Please let's not phone Dominic until I get there and have some idea of what's going on."

If Zane hadn't confided in her about Dominic's fear for Hannah, Meg wouldn't have taken her friend's pleading seriously. Under the circumstances she agreed that it would be better to wait to tell him. Hannah shouldn't have to be worried about calming down Dominic when she needed to conserve her strength for the baby.

"I tell you what. I'm going to call our apartment on the cell phone and ask Zane to drive to yours. He can tend Johnny and Elizabeth so Dominic will be free to join us at the hospital. All right?"

"Yes. Tha— Oh, wow!"

Meg drove faster than usual along the road leading to the freeway. While she cruised down the highway, she talked to her husband who assured her he was on his way to Dom's with Johnny as they spoke.

As they pulled into the hospital's ER entrance, to her surprise and relief Alik greeted them with a wheelchair.

"Just as I was leaving the trailer, Zane phoned us. We decided I would come over here and lend support while Zane brings Dominic. Blaire already left for the apartment to tend all the children."

"Thank you all for your help," Hannah murmured.

"That's what friends are for," he assured her as he assisted her from the car to the wheelchair. Meg drove around to the public parking area, then hurried inside and gave as much information as she could to the triage nurse in reception.

Alik came to find her. "Fortunately Hannah's doctor happens to be in the hospital finishing up another delivery. This couldn't have been timed better.

They're taking her upstairs to the labor and delivery floor right now.''

"Why don't you go with her? I'll stay here and wait for Zane and Dominic.''

"Okay.''

Not two minutes later a white-faced Dominic strode into the ER with Zane. He could be the poster man for the expectant father of the year.

"Meg—''

They embraced. "Your wife is fine, Dominic. Come on. She's upstairs.''

"Already?'' His voice shook.

Zane caught her around the waist and kissed the side of her neck. "Let's pray this doesn't take too long or we'll have to admit Dom,'' he whispered.

"You go with him. I'll phone Blaire and see how things are going with the children. Then I'll join you.''

"Hurry.''

He gave her another kiss on the cheek before catching up with Dominic.

Punching in the digits, she rang Hannah's number and waited for Blaire to pick up.

"Hello?''

"Hi!''

"Meg—did Dominic make it?''

"Yes, but he's about ready to fall apart. Luckily Hannah's coming fast.''

"Thank heaven. I thought he was going to faint on his way out to the car with Zane. Have you ever seen an expectant father act like this before?''

"You'd be surprised how common it is, but I must admit Dom's about the worst case I've witnessed.''

"We want to try for another baby next year. Since

Alik wasn't with me the first time, I hope this doesn't put him off the idea.''

"Of course it won't, but I can tell you right now Zane couldn't be happier he'll never have to watch me go through this.''

Blaire chuckled. "I don't doubt it for a second.''

"How's our little people menagerie?''

"They're fine.''

"Thanks for being such an angel. Hannah's water broke at the stable. That was it!''

"It seems like we've been waiting for this an awfully long time.''

"It's Dominic's fault,'' Meg quipped.

"You're right. Hannah says he's been so broody the last couple of days, they've come close to having their first real quarrel. He refused to go anywhere, even outside! Every time she had to go to the bathroom, he would follow her to make sure she was all right.''

"Yup. That would drive you around the bend.''

"Well, I'm glad I'm not at the hospital to see it.''

"That's why I'm still downstairs in the ER. I figured the guys can handle him a lot better if they're alone with him.''

"There'll be plenty of time after the baby's born to come over and visit her.''

"Agreed. I'll keep you posted.''

Meg clicked off. Before she went upstairs her gaze flicked around the emergency room. The life of the ER was very familiar to her, but she was thankful she was only passing through.

When she joined her husband upstairs, Dom had already been summoned into the birthing room.

She smiled up at her husband. "It won't be long now.''

He looked like he was in terrific form. Alik seemed a little grim. She put her arm through his.

"Are you all right?"

"I've been thinking about Blaire. She had to go through this all alone."

"Her family was there, and you'll be with her next time."

"You can count on it."

Ten minutes went by. Suddenly they saw the door open and the pediatrician emerged with a howling newborn, followed by a nurse and then Dominic. They were headed across the hall for the other room where they could examine the baby.

When he saw them he cried, "Hannah's wonderful! She gave me a daughter. Seven pounds. We're going to call her Gabrielle!" Tears ran down his cheeks before he disappeared.

"Thank heaven that's over!" the three of them said at the same time before they hugged each other for joy.

Alik pulled out his cell phone. "I've got to phone Blaire so she can celebrate with us."

Meg listened as he greeted his wife. "Darling? I have wonderful news. Peace reigns once again on the Wyoming prairie. They have their little Gaby, and God is in his heaven."

It's hard to resist the lure of the Australian Outback

One of Harlequin Romance's best-loved Australian authors

Margaret Way

brings you

Look for

A WIFE AT KIMBARA (#3595)
March 2000

THE BRIDESMAID'S WEDDING (#3607)
June 2000

THE ENGLISH BRIDE (#3619)
September 2000

Available at your favorite retail outlet.

HARLEQUIN®
Makes any time special.™

Visit us at www.romance.net   HROUT

NEARLYWEDS

Almost at the altar— will these *nearlyweds* become *newlyweds*?

Harlequin Romance® is delighted to invite you to some special weddings! Yet these are no ordinary weddings. Our beautiful brides and gorgeous grooms only *nearly* make it to the altar—before fate intervenes.

But the story doesn't end there.... Find out what happens in these tantalizingly emotional novels!

Authors to look out for include:

Leigh Michaels—The Bridal Swap
Liz Fielding—His Runaway Bride
Janelle Denison—The Wedding Secret
Renee Roszel—Finally a Groom
Caroline Anderson—The Impetuous Bride

Available wherever Harlequin books are sold.

HARLEQUIN®
Makes any time special ™

Visit us at www.eHarlequin.com   HRNEAR

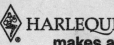

HARLEQUIN®
makes any time special—online...

eHARLEQUIN.com

your romantic
books

♥ Shop online! Visit Shop eHarlequin and discover a wide selection of new releases and classic favorites at great discounted prices.

♥ Read our daily and weekly Internet exclusive serials, and participate in our interactive novel in the reading room.

♥ Ever dreamed of being a writer? Enter your chapter for a chance to become a featured author in our Writing Round Robin novel.

• • • • • •

your romantic
life

♥ Check out our feature articles on dating, flirting and other important romance topics and get your daily love dose with tips on how to keep the romance alive every day.

• • • • • •

your
community

♥ Have a Heart-to-Heart with other members about the latest books and meet your favorite authors.

♥ Discuss your romantic dilemma in the Tales from the Heart message board.

your romantic
escapes

♥ Learn what the stars have in store for you with our daily Passionscopes and weekly Erotiscopes.

♥ Get the latest scoop on your favorite royals in Royal Romance.

HINTA1

If you enjoyed what you just read,
then we've got an offer you can't resist!

Take 2 bestselling
love stories FREE!
Plus get a FREE surprise gift!

Clip this page and mail it to Harlequin Reader Service®

IN U.S.A.	IN CANADA
3010 Walden Ave.	P.O. Box 609
P.O. Box 1867	Fort Erie, Ontario
Buffalo, N.Y. 14240-1867	L2A 5X3

YES! Please send me 2 free Harlequin Romance® novels and my free surprise gift. Then send me 6 brand-new novels every month, which I will receive months before they're available in stores. In the U.S.A., bill me at the bargain price of $2.90 plus 25¢ delivery per book and applicable sales tax, if any*. In Canada, bill me at the bargain price of $3.34 plus 25¢ delivery per book and applicable taxes**. That's the complete price and a savings of 10% off the cover prices—what a great deal! I understand that accepting the 2 free books and gift places me under no obligation ever to buy any books. I can always return a shipment and cancel at any time. Even if I never buy another book from Harlequin, the 2 free books and gift are mine to keep forever. So why not take us up on our invitation. You'll be glad you did!

186 HEN C4GY
386 HEN C4GZ

Name	(PLEASE PRINT)	
Address	Apt.#	
City	State/Prov.	Zip/Postal Code

* Terms and prices subject to change without notice. Sales tax applicable in N.Y.
** Canadian residents will be charged applicable provincial taxes and GST.
   All orders subject to approval. Offer limited to one per household.
® are registered trademarks of Harlequin Enterprises Limited.

HROM00_R2   ©1998 Harlequin Enterprises Limited

Harlequin proudly brings you

STELLA CAMERON
Bobby Hutchinson
Sandra Marton

in

MARRIED IN SPRING

a brand-new anthology in which three couples find that when spring arrives, romance soon follows...along with an unexpected walk down the aisle!

February 2001

Available wherever Harlequin books are sold.

HARLEQUIN®
Makes any time special ™

Visit us at www.eHarlequin.com   PHMARRIED